19

SUGAR CREEK GANG
The GREEN TENT MYSTERY

Paul Hutchens

MOODY PRESS
CHICAGO

Original Title: *The Green Tent Mystery at Sugar Creek*

ISBN: 0-8024-7023-8

3 5 7 9 10 8 6 4 2

Printed in the United States of America

PREFACE

Hi—from a member of the Sugar Creek Gang!

It's just that I don't know which one I am. When I was good, I was Little Jim. When I did bad things—well, sometimes I was Bill Collins or even mischievous Poetry.

You see, I am the daughter of Paul Hutchens, and I spent many an hour listening to him read his manuscript as far as he had written it that particular day. I went along to the north woods of Minnesota, to Colorado, and to the various other places he would go to find something different for the Gang to do.

Now the years have passed—more than fifty, actually. My father is in heaven, but the Gang goes on. All thirty-six books are still in print and now are being updated for today's readers with input from my five children, who also span the decades from the '50s to the '70s.

The real Sugar Creek is in Indiana, and my father and his six brothers were the original Gang. But the idea of the books and their ministry were and are the Lord's. It is He who keeps the Gang going.

PAULINE HUTCHENS WILSON

1

The night we accidentally stumbled onto a brand-new mystery at Sugar Creek was the darkest summer night I ever saw.

Imagine coming happily home with two of your best pals, carrying a string of seven fish and feeling wonderful and proud. And then, halfway home, when you are passing an old abandoned cemetery, imagine seeing a light out there and somebody digging! All of a sudden you get a creeping sensation in your spine, and your hair under your straw hat starts to try to stand up!

Well, that's the way it started. Nobody from Sugar Creek had been buried in that old cemetery for years and years. It was only good for wild strawberries to grow in and bumblebees to make their nest in and barefoot boys to have their gang meetings in, telling ghost stories to each other.

And yet there it was, as plain as the crooked nose on Dragonfly's thin face, or the wide nose on Poetry's face, or the freckled nose on mine —an honest-to-goodness man was digging in the light of a kerosene lantern. The lantern itself was standing beside the tall tombstone of Sarah Paddler, Old Man Paddler's dead wife. It was shedding a spooky light on the man and his nervous movements as he scooped yellowish-brown dirt out of the hole and piled it onto a fast-growing pile beside him.

I knew he couldn't see us, because we were crouched behind some elder bushes that grew along the rail fence just outside the cemetery. But I also knew that if we made the slightest noise he might hear us. And if he heard us—well, what would he do?

I kept hoping Dragonfly's nose, which as everybody knows is almost always allergic to almost everything, wouldn't smell something that would make him sneeze. Dragonfly had the craziest sneeze of anybody in the world—a small squeal with a whistling tail on it. If Dragonfly would sneeze, it would be like the story of Peter Rabbit running away from Mr. McGregor.

As you remember, Peter Rabbit was running *lickety-sizzle*, trying to get away from Mr. McGregor, the gardener. Spying a large sprinkling can, Peter jumped into it to hide himself. The can happened to have water in the bottom, and that was too bad for poor Peter Rabbit's nose. He sneezed, and Mr. McGregor heard it, and Peter had to jump his wet-footed, wet-furred self out of the can and go racing furiously to get away from mad Mr. McGregor and his garden rake.

"Listen," Poetry hissed beside me.

I listened but couldn't hear a thing except the scooping sounds the shovel was making.

Then he squeezed my arm so tight I almost said "Ouch" just as I heard a new sound. It sounded as if the shovel had struck something hard.

"He's struck a rock," I said.

"Rock nothing," Poetry answered. "I'd know that sound anywhere. That was metal scraping on metal or maybe somebody's old coffin."

Poetry's nearly always squawking voice broke when he said that, and he sounded like a frog with laryngitis.

As you know, Dragonfly was the one who was a little more afraid of a cemetery than the rest. So when Poetry said that like that, Dragonfly said, "Let's get out of here! Let's go home!"

Well, I had read different stories about buried treasure. In fact, our own gang had stumbled onto a buried treasure mystery when we were on a camping trip up North and which you can read about in some of the other Sugar Creek Gang books. So when I was peeking through the foliage of the elder bush and between the rails of the tumbledown old fence, watching strange things in a graveyard at a strange hour of the night—well, all of a sudden I was all set to get myself tangled up in another mystery just as quick as I could, that is, if I could without getting into too much danger at the same time. As Dad says, "It is better to have good sense and try to use it than it is to be brave."

Just that second I heard a bobwhite whistling, *"Bob White! Bob White! Poor Bob White!"* It was a very cheery birdcall, the kind I would almost rather hear around Sugar Creek than any other.

As fast as a firefly's fleeting flash, my mind's eye was seeing a ten-inch-long, brown-beaked bird with a white stomach and a white forehead. The feathers on the crown of its head were shaped like the topknot on a topknotted chicken.

The man kept shoveling, not paying attention to anything except what he was doing. He seemed to be working faster though. Then all of a sudden he stopped while he was in a stooped-over position and for a minute didn't make a move.

"He's looking at something in the hole," Poetry whispered. "He sees something."

"Maybe he's listening," I said. It seemed he was—the way a robin does on our front lawn with her head cocked to one side, waiting to see or hear or both a night crawler push part of itself out of its hole. Then she makes a dive for the worm and holds on for dear life while she yanks and pulls till she gets its slimy body out. Then she eats it or else pecks it to death and into small pieces and flies with it to her nest to feed it to her babies.

Seconds later I heard another birdcall, and it was another whistling sound, a very mournful cry. *"Coo-oo, coo-oo, coo-oo."* It was a turtledove.

And it was just as though that sad, plaintive turtledove call had scared the living daylights out of the man. He straightened up, looked all around, picked up the lantern, and started walking toward the old maple tree on the opposite side of the cemetery.

"He's got a limp," Poetry said. "Look how he drags one foot after him."

I didn't have time to wrack my brain to see if I could remember anybody who had that kind of limp. No sooner had the man reached the maple tree than he lifted the lantern and blew out the light.

Then I heard a car door slam and the sound of a motor starting, and two headlights lit up the whole cemetery for a second. Two long, blinding beams made a wide sweep across the top of Strawberry Hill, lighting up the tombstones and the lonely old pine tree above Sarah Paddler's grave and the chokecherry shrubs and even the elder bush we were hiding behind. Then the car went racing down the abandoned lane that led to the road not more than three blocks away, leaving us three boys wondering, *What on earth?* and, *Why?* and, *Who?* and, *Where?*

It seemed I couldn't move—I had been crouched in such a cramped position for so long a time.

It was Dragonfly who thought of something that added to the mystery. He said, "First time I ever heard a bobwhite whistling in the night like that."

The very second he said it, I wished I had thought of it first. But I did think of something else first. Anyway, I said it first. It was, "Yeah, and whoever heard of a *turtledove* cooing in the night?"

"It's just plain cuckoo," Poetry said. "I'll bet there was somebody over there in that car waiting for him and maybe watching, and those whistles meant something special. They probably meant 'Danger! Look out! Get away quick!'"

Then Poetry said in an authoritative voice, as if he were the leader of our gang instead of Big Jim, who is when he is with us—and I am when Big Jim isn't—"Let's go take a look at what he was doing."

"Let's go home," Dragonfly said.

"Why, Dragonfly Gilbert!" I said. "Go on home yourself if you are scared! Poetry and I have got to investigate!"

"I'm not s–scared," Dragonfly said.

As quick as we were sure the car was really gone, I turned on my dad's big long flashlight, and Poetry, Dragonfly, and I started to climb through the rail fence to go toward the mound of yellowish-brown earth beside Sarah Paddler's tombstone.

2

As I said, the three of us started to climb through the rail fence to go to the hole in the ground and investigate what had been going on there. It took us only seconds to get through the fence. Poetry squeezed himself through first, since he is almost twice as big around as either Dragonfly or me. If he could get through, we knew we could, too.

I carried the flashlight, Dragonfly the string of seven fish, and Poetry carried himself. To get to the mound of earth, we had to wind our way around among chokecherry shrubs, wild rosebushes with reddish roses on them, mullein stalks, and different kinds of wildflowers such as blue vervain and especially ground ivy. I noticed it had a lot of dark purple flowers on it—the same color as the vervain. The ground ivy flower clusters were scattered among the heart-shaped leaves of the vine.

Soon we were there, and the three of us, in the form of a right-angle triangle, were standing around the hole. An imaginary line running from Poetry to me made the hypotenuse of the triangle, I thought, and another imaginary line running from Dragonfly to me would make the base.

There wasn't a thing to see in the hole

except a lot of fresh dirt. In fact, there wasn't a thing of any interest whatever to a guy like Poetry, who was the kind of boy who was always looking for a clue of some kind—and especially a mystery—to jump out at him the way a jack-in-the-box does when you press a spring.

The only thing that happened while we were standing half-scared in the silence, looking down into the hole and at the mound of yellowish-brown earth, was that all of a sudden a big beetle came zooming out of the darkness and landed *wham-ety-sizzle-ker-plop* against the side of my freckled face. It bounced off and landed upside down on the yellowish-brown earth, where it began wriggling and twisting and trying to get off its back and onto its six spiny-looking legs.

Anybody who knows anything about bugs and beetles knows that a june bug isn't a bug but is a beetle. It has two different names, one of them being a June beetle and the other a May beetle, depending upon whichever month of the year it flies around in the country where you live.

I was searching every corner of my mind to see if I could imagine that anything I was seeing was a clue to help us solve the new mystery that we had just discovered. Who in the world was the man, and why had he been here? Why had he gotten scared when he heard the bob-white and the turtledove?

I was also remembering that June beetles get awfully hungry at night, and they eat the foliage of oak and willow and poplar trees. In the daytime they hide themselves in the soil of anybody's pasture or in the grass in the woods. June beetles are also crazy about lights at night. The very minute they see one, they make a beetle-line for it just like the beetle that right that second was struggling on its back on the mound of earth.

"Crazy old June beetle!" I said, and Poetry answered, "June *what*?"

"Crazy old June *beetle*," I said, shining my flashlight directly on it and pushing the light up close to its brown body so that Poetry and Dragonfly could see what I was talking about.

Poetry in a disgusted voice said, "When are you going to get over that buggy idea of studying insects?"

I knew I might get over it almost anytime, as I generally do some new hobby that I pick up in the summer. But I didn't want anybody to make fun of the fun I was having studying insects. Dad and I were having more fun that summer than you could shake a stick at, catching different kinds of insects, especially beetles, which anybody knows have four wings. The two wings in front are not used for flying but are like a hard rainproof roof protecting its two flying wings. Those, when the beetle isn't flying, are all nicely folded up underneath like two colored umbrellas.

Little Jim was always collecting things, too, and he was to blame for inspiring me to start a collection of my own. That summer he was looking up different kinds of wild flowers and writing their names in a notebook. But that week Dad and I were studying beetles.

Just that minute the big brown beetle I had my flashlight focused on wriggled itself off the clod of dirt and went *tumblety-sizzle* down the side of the mound and landed *ker-plop* in the grave itself.

"Poor little scarab beetle," I said to it. "I'll bet that right this very second one of your nearest relatives is in that great big yellow-stomached catfish I caught a half hour ago at the mouth of the branch."

Anybody knows that one of the best baits in the world to catch a catfish at night is a juicy grub worm, which is a little C-shaped larva that hatches out of the egg of an insect such as a June beetle.

"You'd be scared, too," Poetry said, "if you were flying around at night and saw a light in a cemetery accidentally and all of a sudden found yourself right in the bottom of a newly dug grave."

"Poetry," I said, "I didn't say *scared*. I said *scarab*." Then, feeling kind of proud of all the different things Dad and I had learned that week, I began to rattle off some of it to Poetry. "That's what kind of beetle it is," I said. "Only it doesn't eat dead stuff like some scarab beetles do. Its larvae eat the roots of nearly everything Dad plants in our new ground, but most scarabs eat dead things and worse stuff."

"Cut out the education!" Poetry said. "Who

cares about that? I suppose you think that's why he flew into this old cemetery in the first place. He was looking for something dead to eat. Maybe that's why he dived headfirst into the side of your face!"

"Cut it out, yourself," I said, feeling a little temper-fire starting in my mind.

Just then the June beetle unscrambled himself or herself, spread his shell-like front wings and his reddish-brown back wings and took off again, straight in the direction of my face. But I snapped off the flashlight quick and ducked my head, and he missed me and disappeared into the night, on his way, maybe, to the lighted window of somebody's house. If he should happen to see one somewhere, and if there should be a window open without a screen, some woman or girl would soon be screaming bloody murder for a man or boy to come and save her life.

"Turn your light on again, quick!" Dragonfly said. "Let's get out of here!" He quickly started to do it himself, but we stopped him.

We looked all around everywhere but still couldn't find a single clue to tell why whoever he was had been digging there.

"Hey!" Poetry exclaimed excitedly all of a sudden. "Here's a clear shoe print in the soft dirt!"

Then, as if he had seen a ghost, he almost screamed as he said, "It's a *woman's* high-heeled shoe!"

What on earth? I thought.

"But it was a m–m–man digging!" Dragon-fly stammered.

"Then it was a woman dressed in overalls!" I said in the most excited voice I had heard myself use in a long time.

I stooped and shoved Dad's powerful flashlight down next to the neat little shoe print. "She had very small feet," I said.

Naturally, there wasn't anything extramysterious about a woman wearing overalls or jeans around Sugar Creek, especially when she was doing the kind of hard work that men have to do and some women have to do sometimes. But what would a woman be doing digging in an abandoned cemetery late at night?

"What on earth?" I said.

Not a one of us knew what to do or say next, so we decided to go over to the old maple tree. The minute we got there, Poetry ordered me to shine my light around the tree trunk while he studied the bark to see if any of it had been freshly knocked off.

"What are you looking for?" I asked.

"To see if a *human* bobwhite or a *human* turtledove was hiding up there among the branches as a sort of lookout for the woman. Those two bird whistles were warnings of some kind."

What he said made sense, but we couldn't stay all night, and our six parents would be wondering why we didn't come home—and also worrying. Any boy who has good sense doesn't like to do any dumb thing to make his parents worry any more than they would do anyway. A parent is something a boy would have a hard time doing without, especially when it is time for breakfast or dinner or supper. Besides, who would give him a licking when he needed it, which every once in a while he probably does?

So we decided to go on home, get secret word to the rest of the gang—Big Jim, Circus, Little Jim, and Little Tom Till—to all meet us at the pine tree beside Sarah Paddler's tombstone tomorrow right after lunch. Then we could look to see if together we could find out what had been going on: why a limping woman in overalls was digging in an old abandoned cemetery, and who had given the bobwhite and turtledove calls and why.

"Let's go home and get some sleep," I said to Dragonfly and Poetry. We would go up the lane to the highway, following the old brown path that, twenty minutes ago, the car had followed.

Then what to my wondering ears should come, from back in the direction *of* the open grave and Sarah Paddler's tombstone, but a quail's sharp, clear call. *"Bob White! Bob White! Poor Bob White!"*

Dragonfly, who had been standing there under the tree with us, his teeth chattering, jumped as if a firecracker had exploded under him. He whirled into fast life, and a second later his spindly legs were flying like a June beetle's wings, carrying him up the lane toward the road that would lead us home.

As fast as two other firecrackers getting exploded from the explosion of the first one, Poetry and I dashed madly after him. The faster I ran, the more scared I got. We didn't stop until, panting and gasping for breath, we got to my house.

Well, at the very second we came panting into our yard and up to the iron pitcher pump at the end of the board walk about twenty feet from our back door, Dad came sauntering up from the direction of the barn. He was carrying a kerosene lantern and—would you believe it? —*a spade and a shovel!*

"Wh–what are you doing?" I said, still panting and a little mixed up in my mind.

"Oh, just digging around in the earth a little," Dad said in a lazy, yawning voice. "Been burying something or other."

Three boys looked at each other from three different directions and felt terribly disappointed, for it looked as if our mystery was going to explode right in front of our worried faces.

"Somebody die?" Poetry asked, trying to be mischievous at a time when he shouldn't have.

Dad said indifferently, "Just a couple of newborn pigs. Old Red Addie gave us a new family of eight tonight. Two of them didn't live, so I thought I'd bury them right away."

After our having been half scared to death, here our mystery was all solved, I thought. Or was it? How about the woman's shoe tracks and the mysterious birdcalls and the car?

Well, we divided our seven fish into three parts. Poetry took three sunfish, Dragonfly three, and I took the big catfish, which I myself had caught using the descendant—or else what might have been the ancestor—of a June beetle. That big, yellow-stomached catfish was as big as three sunfish. It was, in fact, as big as all six of the insignificant fish that Dragonfly and Poetry had pulled in after the fish had accidentally hooked themselves onto their merely worm-baited hooks and gotten themselves pulled in to shore.

3

Next day we managed to get the news around quick to all the rest of the gang—but secretly, because it seemed our parents ought not to know what was going on until we ourselves investigated. Anybody knows a mystery isn't a mystery any longer if someone explains it, and there's nobody that can spoil a boy's mystery any quicker than his very bright parents, who always know almost everything anyway—one reason being that our dads used to be boys themselves.

The very second I finished all of my dinner that day, except my piece of apple pie, I looked past Dad's overhanging, reddish-brown eyebrows to where Mom sat at the end of the table. "May I be excused and eat my pie outdoors?" I asked.

You see, if there is anything I would rather do than anything else, it is to leave the table early—before anybody thinks about starting to do the dishes—take my one-sixth of an apple pie, go out our screen door with the pie in one hand and my straw hat in the other, swing out to our grape arbor, step up on a wooden box, reach up, and lay the pie on top of the two-by-four crossbeam at the east end of the arbor, where there isn't any vine growing.

Then, I like to climb up and sit on the top with the cool breeze blowing in my freckled face and my two bare feet with their ten stubby toes swinging below me. I hold the nicely crusted pie upside down and eat it that way, while I look around the Sugar Creek territory to where different members of our gang live. I also like to look at our farm and the barn and the chicken house and the big walnut tree with the long rope swing hanging from the first branch, and the plum tree with the robin's nest in the three-limbed crotch up near the top. Boy oh boy, does it make me feel fine, glad to be alive, and especially glad to be a boy!

Even while I was asking to be excused, I was imagining myself already outdoors, sitting up on the flat side of the two-by-four.

But Dad was as smart as I was—smart enough to read my mind—and he saw things in it that I hardly knew were there. Right that second he looked at Mom and said, "There are some good habits, some bad habits, and some that are in between. The ones in between don't hurt a boy very much, but they help to make him *him.*

"And that's getting to be quite a habit with you, Bill," he finished, looking at me with his gray-green eyes.

I had been looking at the pie, which I already had in my hand, expecting Mom to say yes, as she nearly always does.

"What habit?" I said innocently.

"Use plain American, Theodore," Mom

said to Dad. "The boy doesn't understand philosophy."

And Dad said to Mom, with a mischievous twinkle in his eye, "May I take my pie and go outdoors and eat it upside down on top of our grape arbor?"

Mom looked up at him with a sort of quizzical expression on her face. There was also a twinkle in her eye that seemed funny to Dad but not to me. Then she said, "Certainly. You can do that while Bill and I do the dishes."

Dad said, "Thank you." Then he took *his* one-sixth of a pie in his big, hard, suntanned farmer hand and slipped out of his chair and outdoors fast. He let the screen slam hard behind him the way I sometimes do—and shouldn't. Outside, he let out a bloodcurdling war whoop, and I heard his footsteps running toward the grape arbor.

A second later I was outdoors too.

Now, if there is anything that looks ridiculous, it is a boy's long-legged, red-haired, bushy-eyebrowed father grunting himself into an upside-down knot and out of it again while he climbs up onto a high grape arbor.

But a jiffy later, there was Dad up there where I should have been, with his heavy work shoes on his large feet swinging, and eating his pie upside down, and panting for breath from all the unnecessary exercise.

It was funny to Dad, but to me it looked silly. So I sat down on the porch with my back to him and ate my pie right side up, and for some reason it didn't taste very good.

It was a scorching hot day, and I was beginning to feel a little better there in the shade, when all of a sudden Mom said from inside the house, using a very cheerful voice, "OK, Bill. The dishes are all ready for you."

I always know, when Mom calls me cheerfully like that, that she's trying to make me *want* to come.

But Dad turned out to be a really neat dad after all, or else he was trying to give me a free education. It seemed he was still pretending to be me up there on that grape arbor, so when he heard Mom say "dishes," he called out cheerfully, "Coming," and quickly swung around and down off the grape arbor and hurried into the house as if he would rather dry the Collins family dinner dishes than do anything else in the whole world.

He got stopped at the door by Mom, though, who was maybe trying to play the game with him. She said, "Wipe that dirt off your shoes on the mat there"—which she tells me about thirty-seven times a day, sometimes even while I am already doing it, having thought of it first myself.

I looked at Dad's feet, and they did have dirt on them—*a yellowish brown dirt on the sides of the soles and heels!*

At the very second I saw Dad's shoes with that dirt on them instead of the very black dirt I knew was the kind that was under the pignut trees, I wondered, *What on earth?* I certainly didn't want my dad to be getting mixed up in our mystery, as I had thought for a minute last night he might be.

Not only that, I didn't want him to have been the person who had given the bobwhite and turtledove birdcalls, which my discouraged mind was trying to tell me he could have been.

Not knowing I was going to say what I did, I said, *"Dad!"* in a loud and astonished voice. "*Where* did you get that kind of mud on your shoes?" I was using the kind of voice I had heard another member of our family use on me several different times in my life.

Dad, who was already wiping his shoes on the mat at the door, looked down at them and said, "What dirt?"

Mom's astonished voice shot through the screen door. "Why, Theodore Collins! What on *earth!*"

Dad grinned back through the screen at her and said, "No, not *what on earth* but *earth on what?*" which I could tell he thought was funny.

Mom didn't think it was, very. She went on in her same astonished, accusing voice. "Those are the very same muddy shoes you ate dinner with!"

"I never ate dinner with muddy shoes in my life," Dad said with a grin in his voice. "I always use a knife and fork and spoon," which was supposed to be extrafunny, and it was to Dad and me, but for some reason Mom only smiled rather than laughed and looked as though she was trying to keep herself from even smiling.

"Go get your father's house slippers," she ordered me, and I obeyed her in a hurry.

Dad slipped his feet out of his shoes and left them on the porch. Then he put his feet into his slippers and ordered me to follow him into the house, which I also did with a little less speed, because I could tell by the tone of his voice that he had some work for me to do, which I found out was the truth.

It wasn't too bad though, for Dad and I played a little game while we did the dishes. He called me "Dad," and I called him "Bill." He also ordered Mom to go into the front room to look after my baby sister, Charlotte Ann.

Well, we dived headfirst—or rather, hands first—into the sudsy dishwater and made short work of those dishes, getting them done a lot faster than if a mother and daughter had done them. Also we hurried to be sure to get through before Mom might come out into the kitchen and look over our work and decide we were not using the right kind of soap or something.

It really was fun. I kept giving orders to my red-haired, awkward son, giving him commands every few minutes, such as "Keep your mind on your work, Bill!" and "Hey, that plate has to be wiped over again!" or "Your mother likes to have the glasses polished a little better than that, son. We never know when there might be company from somewhere and those glasses have to shine like everything"—unnecessary things a father nearly always says to a boy.

Well, those dishes got done in about half the usual time.

As soon as they were finished, I thought I was free to start to do what I really wanted to do in just the way I wanted to do it, but I got stopped by Dad's big, gruff voice. I had just tossed the drying towel toward the rack beside the stove. I missed the rack and made a dive to pick it up quickly before Dad, or especially Mom, might see it. I was still in a bent-over position—just right for a good spank from somebody—when Dad's voice socked me. His words were "Which one of us is Bill, and which is your father now—for the rest of the afternoon, I mean?"

"I am," I said. In a second the towel was on the rack, nice and straight, and I was over by the washstand, stooping to get my straw hat, which was beside Dad's big work shoes.

"Bring the gang home sometime this afternoon," Dad said. "I want to show them Addie's nice, new red-haired family."

"I will," I answered, having seen the six cute little quadrupeds myself that morning.

By that time I was already outdoors and ten feet from the slammed screen door. The door had slammed itself because of a strong coiled spring.

Then Dad called again and stopped me stock-still. "If I am your father again and you are Bill Collins, you had better stay home and mow the lawn and let me go to meet the gang."

But I could tell he didn't mean it. Dad looked awfully cute, I thought, with Mom's big apron on, his blue shirt sleeves rolled up to the elbows, and his slippers still on, standing in the open screen door.

I called back saying, "I am still Theodore Collins, and you are Bill, and you are letting flies in. Shut the door quick—and *quietly!*"

As I hurried away, my mischievous dad called after me, "So long, Mr. Collins! Have a nice time, and don't forget to find a new beetle for our collection."

"So long, Bill!" I yelled from the front gate, which I had just opened and gone through and shut after me.

Then, as I dashed past "Theodore Collins" on our mailbox, I was myself again. I swished across the dusty road and vaulted over the lichen-covered rail fence. Soon I was running in the path that had been made by barefoot boys, down through the woods as fast as I could go to the spring, where the gang was going to meet before going up to the top of Strawberry Hill to the cemetery.

4

Boy oh boy! I never felt better in my life than I did when I was galloping through that woods to meet the gang. First I was in the sunlight and then in the shade as I raced along on that winding little brown path, swishing by maple, beech, ash, and oak trees and dodging chokecherry shrubs and wild rosebushes with roses scattered all around among their thorns and dogwood shrubs and all kinds of wildflowers that grew on either side of the path.

Even though I had been delayed unnecessarily because of the dishes, I got to the spring about the same time Little Jim and Poetry did. Circus was already there in his favorite place, where he usually waits for us when he gets there first, which is in the top branches of a little elm sapling that grows at the top of the steep bank. As you know, at the bottom of that bank is the spring itself, but we always meet in a little shaded, open space at the top. Circus was swinging and swaying and looked really like a chimpanzee, hanging by his hands and feet and everything except his tail, which he didn't have anyway.

As soon as Big Jim, with his almost mustache, and Little Tom Till, with his freckled face and red hair, and Dragonfly, with his goggleeyes and spindly legs got there, that was all of us.

Poetry, Dragonfly, and I told everybody what had happened last night, but I didn't tell them about Dad's having had yellowish-brown dirt on his shoes. And with my eyes I kept Poetry and Dragonfly from telling them about the two baby pigs Dad had buried somewhere, because I felt sure Dad wouldn't bury two baby pigs in a cemetery that had been reserved for human beings only.

A little later, after a loafing ramble along the bayou and a climb to the top of Strawberry Hill, we scrambled over the rail fence and reached the place where the woman had been digging last night, not more than ten feet from Sarah Paddler's tombstone. Well, we all stood around in a barefoot circle, looking down into the hole. Sure enough—just as we had seen last night, there was the print of a high-heeled shoe. There were also other high-heeled shoe tracks all around, but none of the others were as clear as the one we were all studying that very minute.

"What on earth do you suppose she was digging here for?" Little Tom Till asked in his high-pitched voice.

Big Jim answered him, saying, "If we knew that, we would know what we want to know."

For a minute I focused my eyes on the hand that somebody had chiseled on Sarah Paddler's tombstone. One finger pointed toward the sky. I had read the words just below the hand maybe a hundred twenty times in my life. They were: "There is rest in heaven," which I knew there was for anybody who got to go there.

When I was in a cemetery, it was easy to think about things like that. I was sort of dreamily remembering that our minister in the Sugar Creek church says there is only one way for a boy to get to heaven. First, the boy has to believe that he is an honest-to-goodness sinner and needs to be saved. Then he has to believe that Jesus, who is the Savior, came all the way from heaven a long time ago to die for him and to save him from his sins. Then if the boy will open the door of his heart and let the Savior come in, that will settle it.

Our minister, who knows many Bible verses by heart, tells the people who come to our church that there isn't any other way for anybody to be saved except just the way I told you.

So I knew that Old Man Paddler, who was saved himself and was the kindest long-whiskered old man that ever was a friend to a boy, would see his wife Sarah again—maybe the very minute he got to heaven.

While I was standing there by the hole the June beetle had tumbled into last night and was looking up at that carved hand on the tombstone, my mind sort of drifted away on a friendly little journey clear up into heaven. It went past the great big white cumulus cloud that right that minute was piling itself up in the southwest above the tree-covered hills where I knew Old Man Paddler's cabin was.

I imagined that somewhere in heaven maybe there was a very nice little cabin waiting for that kind old man, and that his wife, Sarah, was out there in the garden looking after the flowers for him. Every now and then she would stop doing what she was doing and look toward a little white gate, like the one we have at our house by the walnut tree, to see if she could see her husband coming. Then I imagined that all of a sudden she did see him, and her kind, oldish face lit up the way Mom's does sometimes when she sees Dad coming home from somewhere. And she started quickly on a half-walk and half-run out across the heavenly yard to meet him, calling, "Hi there! I've been waiting for you a long time."

It was a terribly nice thought. But I knew that if the old man ever left Sugar Creek, it would be awfully lonesome around here for a long time. It sort of seemed we needed him here even more than his wife did up there.

From Sarah Paddler's grave in the shade of the big pine tree, we went all the way across the cemetery, winding around a little to get to the old maple, where last night we had looked for signs of a human quail or a human turtledove.

There we stopped in the friendly shade and lay down in the tall grass to hold a meeting to help us decide what to do next. While we were lying there in seven different directions, chewing the juicy ends of bluegrass and timothy and wild rye, Big Jim gave a special order, which was: "I would like each of us except Poetry and Dragonfly to give a quail whistle."

"Why?" Tom Till wanted to know.

"I want to find out if any of *you* were out here last night making those calls. I also want to know if any of you guys were out here dressed in overalls and wearing a woman's high-heeled shoes."

Little Jim and Tom Till and Circus and Big Jim himself did the best they could making bobwhite calls, but Circus was the only one of us whose whistle sounded like the quail whistle we had heard last night.

Then Big Jim made all of us except Poetry, Dragonfly, and me do a turtledove call. Again Circus was the only one whose call was like the one we heard last night.

"OK, Circus." Big Jim leveled his eyes across our little tangled-up circle and said to him, "Confess, or we will drag you down to Sugar Creek and throw you in."

"All right," Circus said, "I confess I was home in bed sound asleep when I heard those calls last night."

"So was I," Tom Till said.

"So was I," Little Jim echoed.

"Yeah, and so was I. Sound asleep in bed, listening to the calls," Big Jim said sarcastically.

Well, that left only Poetry, Dragonfly, and me, and we were the ones who had heard the calls in the first place, so the mystery was as still unsolved as it had been. Not a one of us believed that Circus was there last night.

There wasn't any use to stay where we were, and since it was a very hot afternoon, we decided to go to the old swimming hole and get cooled off.

"Last one in is a bear's tail," Circus yelled back at us over one of his square shoulders as he galloped off first, across the cemetery to the other side.

The rest of us took off after him, not a one of us wanting to be a bear's tail, which meant we would have to be almost nothing, because bears have very stubby tails.

Long before we got to the creek, nearly every one of us had his shirt off, so that by the time we got there all we would have to do would be to wrestle ourselves out of our overalls. In a jiffy we would be out in the middle of the greatest water for swimming in the whole world. Every one of us knew how to swim like a fish, for our parents had made us learn as soon as we were old enough to—as everybody in the world should.

And then you should have seen the way our mystery began to come to life, even while we were still on the shore before splashing ourselves in.

All of a sudden, Little Jim, who was undressing in the shade of a willow where he always hangs his clothes, yelled in a very excited voice for him, "Hey, Bill! Circus! Poetry! Everybody! Come here quick! Hurry! Look what I found!"

Well, when Little Jim or any of our gang calls in an excited voice like that, it always sends a half-dozen thrills through me, because it nearly always means something extraspecial.

I galloped across to where he was, my shirt in one hand and one of my overall legs in the other, getting there as quick as the rest of us. I also managed to grab up a stick on my way, just in case Little Jim might have spied a water moccasin or some other kind of snake, of which there are maybe twenty different varieties around Sugar Creek.

Little Jim was excitedly pointing down with a right forefinger to something on the little strip of sand at the water's edge.

At first I didn't see a thing except some shaded water where fifty or more small, black, flat whirligig beetles were racing around in circles on the surface. I could smell ripe apples, which is the kind of odor a whirligig beetle gives off. Anybody who knows anything about whirligig beetles knows that smell comes from a kind of milky fluid that they use to protect themselves from being eaten by fish or some kind of water bird or something else.

Even Poetry didn't see what Little Jim was excited about. "Education again," he said with a disgruntled snort and turned back to the swimming hole.

Dragonfly, who wasn't interested in Dad's and my new hobby, grunted, too. Then he sneezed and said, "I'm allergic to the smell of sweet bugs." That is a common name for those lively little ripe-apple-smelling beetles.

"They're whirligig beetles," I said, wanting

to defend Little Jim for calling us over in such an excited voice for what the rest of the gang would think was almost nothing.

"But, look, everybody!" Little Jim yelled. "Look! See, it's a clue!"

Then my eyes went in the direction his finger was really pointing, and I saw what he saw. A thrill started whirligigging in my very surprised brain, for what to my wondering eyes did appear but, half hidden in the grass, a pair of women's new shoes—very small, expensive-looking white pumps with extrahigh heels and a design across the toes that looked kind of like the leaves from the ground ivy growing all around Sarah Paddler's tombstone.

What on earth! I thought. I remembered that Dad had said, *"Earth on what?"* when I saw there were some yellowish brown earth stains on those extrahigh heels of those new-looking women's shoes.

Just that second Dragonfly said, *"Psst!* Listen," which everybody did. And there it was again, as plain as a Sugar Creek cloudless day. A sharp bobwhite call from down the creek somewhere: *"Bob White! Bob White! Poor Bob White!"*

5

If that bobwhite call was from a real quail, then we didn't have anything to worry about. But we all knew that honest-to-goodness quails not only don't make their very pretty calls in the middle of the night, but also they don't do it in the middle of a sultry, sunny midsummer afternoon. Or if they do, I didn't remember having heard any do it around Sugar Creek. And if it had been a human being calling like a quail, then what?

If it was a *man* human being, we would all want to scramble ourselves out of there and hide somewhere, so that whoever he was wouldn't see us. But if it was a *woman* human being who had made the quail call—which it might have been, I thought, because some woman's shoes were lying right this minute in the sand beside Little Jim—then every single one of us ought to make a headfirst dive toward getting his clothes on.

Before we could start to decide what to do, we heard the quail call again. This time it was a lot nearer than it had been. In fact, it sounded as if it wasn't a hundred feet distant and had come from the direction of the spring, from which we ourselves had just come. That meant that the person, man *or* woman, was maybe walking on the same path we had been running on a little while before. We wouldn't have even half-enough time to get our clothes on before running to hide.

I looked all around our tense circle to see if the rest of the gang had any ideas as to what to do, and it seemed not a one of us could do a thing except stand still with his eyes and ears glued to the direction from which the last quail call had come.

"Quick, Dragonfly!" I heard myself say, taking charge of things. "Get those shoes, quick, and let's get out of here!" I shouldn't have done that, because Big Jim is our leader when he is with us.

And Big Jim took my leadership away from me in a split second by saying, "Leave those shoes alone! Don't you dare touch them! If anything has happened, we don't want our fingerprints on them!"

And then we were scrambling up the slope, leaving those shoes about eighteen inches from the whirligig beetles, and with all our minds whirligigging like everything—some of us with our clothes half on and others with them half off and the rest of the gang with them all off. We were getting ourselves out of there fast.

At the top of the little slope, we came to the narrow footpath, zipped across it, and disappeared into the tall corn of one of Dragonfly's dad's cornfields.

I knew that on the opposite side of that narrow strip of cornfield was the bayou. It was divided into two parts, having a long pond on either end, and each of those ponds had in it some very lazy water in which there were a few mud pickerel, or barred pickerel, as some people call them. Between the two ponds was a strip of soggy, marshy soil and a little path that was bordered by giant ragweeds. This was a sort of shortcut to the woods from the old swimming hole.

Once we got to the woods, we could follow the rail fence as we had done last night and come out at the place where Little Jim had killed the bear. You have probably read about that in one of the other Sugar Creek Gang stories. As you know, that was at the bottom of Strawberry Hill. And at the top of the hill were the old cemetery and the hole in the ground beside Sarah Paddler's tombstone.

There we would be safe if whoever was coming up that path, nearer and nearer every second, was dangerous.

As quickly as we were far enough into the tall corn to be hidden from sight of the path, we dropped down on the ground to listen and to see if we could learn what was going on. As you know, corn blades are not as thick at the bottom of the stalks as they are at the top, so if anybody came up the path, we could see his feet if we were lying on the ground.

Poetry, lying close to me, whispered in my ear, "*Shh!* There he is!"

I looked and saw the cuffs of somebody's

trousers standing at the end of my corn row in the very place where we always left the path to dive down the incline into our willow-protected outdoor dressing room. Then came a startling quail call again, and this time it sounded so near that it almost scared me out of what few wits I hadn't already been scared out of.

I waited, wondering if there would be an answer. And then what to my astonished ears should come but the sound of a turtledove's low, sad, lonesome call from farther up the path.

Almost right away I saw the skirt of a woman's yellowish dress coming out of our green dressing room! I also noticed that she was barefoot. Straining my ears, I could hear her talking and complaining about something the way a boy does when he gets called by his mother to leave his play. I could hear the man's voice too, but I couldn't make out what he was saying.

Then I heard her say, "I was having so much fun wading in the riffles. Look! I found this—a big washboard shell! I'll bet I'll find a pearl in it! Wouldn't it be wonderful if I did find one worth hundreds of dollars?"

And I heard the man say, "That's fine, but it's time for your rest. Let's get back to the tent."

So! They were camping somewhere up in Old Man Paddler's woods. That meant they would either have to get their drinking water at the spring, where our gang met every day when our parents would let us, or they would have to come to *our* house to get it out of the iron pitcher pump at the end of the board walk near our back door and grape arbor.

For some reason that didn't make me feel very good. Of course, Old Man Paddler owned nearly all the territory around Sugar Creek, and he had the right to let anybody camp on it that he wanted to. Still, it seemed the whole territory belonged to the Sugar Creek Gang, especially the woods around the spring, because our bare feet had walked on nearly every square inch of it. We had climbed nearly every tree and rested in the shade of every one of them. This was too much like having company at our house. You don't feel free to yell and scream and give loon calls and go screeching through the woods, yelling like wild men, or anything, when somebody strange is camping there. You even have to comb your hair when you are outdoors, if there happens to be a city woman around.

I thought and felt all that while we were still lying on the sandy soil of Dragonfly's dad's cornfield and the man and the woman were still not more than a few yards up the path on their way toward the spring.

They were out of hearing distance now, but I could see the movement the tall weeds were making as they swayed back into place after the man and woman went through. The movement was like it is when the wind blows across our wheatfield.

Then they were gone, and I could hear only the sound of the breathing of seven half-dressed, half-undressed boys.

Using my nervous voice, I said, "What on *earth*?" before any of the rest of the gang did.

Circus, trying to be funny, said, "Seven boys are."

We would have to go in swimming now to get the sand of Dragonfly's cornfield off ourselves. Besides I had some dirt in my red hair too, and it would have to be dived out.

It was a not-very-happy gang of boys that sneaked back to our leafy dressing room and then went in swimming.

"Did any of you guys hear him say, 'Let's get back to the tent'?" I asked.

"Sure," Poetry said. "What of it?"

"What of it?" I exclaimed. "Why, that means they are *camping* up there in the woods somewhere, and we'll have to be scared half to death every time we go in swimming for fear some woman and her husband will hear or see us. Or else we'll have to wear swim trunks!" None of our gang had ever worn them in our whole lives.

I had just come up from diving and was shaking the water out of my ears and rubbing it out of my eyes so that I could hear and see, when our mystery came to livelier life than before.

It happened like this. Little Jim was dressing over by the willow where he always dresses and where the whirligig beetles were still in swimming, having a sweet time going round and round on the surface of the water like boys and girls skating on Sugar Creek in the wintertime.

He had just finished shoving his head through the neck of his shirt and was reaching for his overalls that were hanging on the willow when all of a sudden he let out another excited yell. "Hey, Bill! Circus! Poetry! Everybody! Come here quick! Hurry! Look what I found. It's somebody's billfold!"

When I got some of the water out of my ears and eyes and could see, I saw him holding up a pretty brown billfold like the kind Mom carries in her handbag.

Not waiting to finish getting the water out of my ears and eyes, I went *splashety-gallop* straight for Little Jim, who was on the shore by the willow, still holding up the leather billfold for us to see. All the rest of the gang were already splashing their different ways toward him, and almost all of us got there at the same time.

Well, when those black, flat, oval whirligig beetles saw or heard or felt us coming out of our swimming hole toward theirs, they got scared. At once, the way whirligig beetles do when they are badly frightened, they stopped going around in their fast, excited circles and dived under the water to hide themselves on the bottom of Sugar Creek. By the time I got there, there wasn't one in sight, and only the smell of ripe apples was left.

The billfold was made out of a very rich-looking leather that could have been goatskin, although maybe it was what leather workers call saddle leather. It had a pretty tooled design on it, a galloping horse with wings. On the other side of the billfold were the initials F. E.

Now, what do you do with a woman's fancy billfold when you find it on the ground in a boys' outdoor dressing room? Do you open the billfold to see what's in it? Or do you open it just to see what name is on the identification card in one of its windows, which most billfolds have for the owner's name and address and for pictures of favorite friends?

Since Big Jim was the leader of our gang, Little Jim handed the billfold to him, and right away Big Jim said, "It probably belongs to the turtledove that was here a little while ago looking for her high-heeled shoes. We'd better get dressed quick and take out after her and her bobwhite husband or brother. We'll see if we can find her and give the billfold back to her."

"What's her name?" Tom Till wanted to know. He crowded in between Little Jim and me, turning his face sideways so that as soon as Big Jim would open the billfold, he could read the name on the identification card.

"We don't need to know that," Big Jim said, but I noticed he did decide to unzip the zipper. And when he did, the billfold flopped open like a four-page leather-covered book. There were four windows with a picture on each side of three of them. One of the windows had a card, and the name on it was Frances Everhard. Then I got a view of one of the most astonishing surprises I ever had in my life.

Dragonfly, who was closest to Big Jim and looking over his elbow, exclaimed, "Why, she's got a picture of Bill's baby sister!"

You should have seen me crowd my way into the middle of our huddle to Big Jim's side to see what Dragonfly thought he saw. And to my surprise I saw one of the cutest pictures of Charlotte Ann that I had ever seen. In fact, it was one I had *never* seen before, and I wondered when Mom had had it taken and how on earth a barefoot woman who dug holes in a cemetery at night had gotten it.

In the picture, Charlotte Ann was sitting in a fancy high chair that had what looked like an adjustable footrest, the kind they sell in the Sugar Creek Furniture Store. The food tray looked shiny and was maybe made out of chrome. I remembered Mom had once looked at one like that in town and had wanted to buy it for Charlotte Ann, but Dad had said the old one I had used when I was a baby, which was years and years ago, was good enough. It had made a husky boy out of me, and besides he couldn't afford it—the way he can't a lot of things Mom would like to buy and maybe knows she shouldn't, because Dad is still trying to save money so he can buy a new tractor.

Also, Charlotte Ann was wearing a cute baby bonnet and a stylish-looking coat with a lot of lacy stuff around the collar. I didn't remember her having any outfit like that at all, although Mom could have bought it and had her picture taken one day in town when I hadn't known about it.

She certainly had a cute expression on her face, one I had seen her have hundreds of times. It looked as if she was thinking some very mischievous thoughts and was trying to tell somebody what she was thinking and couldn't because she couldn't talk yet.

"It's *not* a picture of Charlotte Ann," Little Jim said, who managed to get his small, curly head in close enough to take a look. "She's got more hair than that."

Circus spoke up then and said, "It was taken when she was a little smaller. She's bigger than that now."

There were other pictures of different people in the billfold. Little Jim noticed there was money in the bill compartment—in fact, three fives and a ten and several ones, each of the ones having on it a picture of George Washington, the first president of the United States; the fives, a picture of Abraham Lincoln; and the ten, one of Andrew Jackson.

Well, we brought it to a quick vote, and the decision was to take the billfold up the path and start looking for the tent the man and the woman were camping in and ask them if they had lost it.

As we moved along in a sort of half-worried hurry up the path toward the spring, I couldn't for the life of me think how on earth the barefoot woman could have gotten a picture of my baby sister. What would she want with it, anyway?

Well, maybe in the next fifteen minutes or so I would find out. But I was worried a little because, even as I followed along behind Poetry —all of us had to walk single file because the path through the tall weeds was just wide enough for one barefoot boy at a time—I was remembering that the woman was probably the same person who last night had been digging a hole in the old cemetery under the big pine tree beside Sarah Paddler's tombstone. I wondered what she had been digging in the earth for.

6

It was a terribly hot, sultry day, and over in the southwest a great big yellowish cumulus cloud was building up into a thunderhead. I knew from having lived around Sugar Creek for years and years that maybe before the day was over we would find ourselves in the middle of a whopper of a thunderstorm. That is the way the southwest part of the sky looks when it is getting ready to pour out about a million gallons of nice clean rainwater all over the farms around Sugar Creek.

Because Charlotte Ann's picture was in the pretty brown billfold, which Big Jim had zipped shut again, he let me carry it, which I did in the pocket of my overalls.

Whew! It was hot and sultry on the footpath to the spring, even though it was mostly shaded. Pretty soon we came to the spring itself, which is at the bottom of an incline and has an old linden tree leaning out over it and shading it. Dad had made a cement reservoir there, which was always full of the clearest water you ever saw. The water itself came singing out of an iron pipe, the other end of which Dad had driven way back into the rocky hillside.

"Here are a woman's tracks again!" Dragonfly said, looking down at the mud on the west side of the spring.

My eyes followed his, expecting to see the print of a woman's high-heeled shoes. Instead, I saw the print of a very small, bare foot with a narrow heel and five small toes, which meant that the woman had still been carrying her shoes when she had walked along here on the way back to her tent.

I also noticed there was a closed glass fruit jar in the spring reservoir with what looked like maybe a pound of yellow butter in it! It was like the kind we churned ourselves at our house, using an old-fashioned dasher churn, which I nearly always had to churn myself. I was even a better churner than Dad. Sometimes Dad would churn for twenty minutes and not get any butter, and I could come in and churn for five minutes and it would be done fast.

That butter in the fruit jar meant that the man and woman were using *our* spring to get their drinking water and also to keep their butter from getting too soft. Mom does that at our house, except that we keep ours in a fruit jar or a crock in the cellar instead.

Anyway, I thought, they wouldn't have to come to our house to get their drinking water out of our iron pitcher pump.

From the spring we went up the incline past the elm sapling, where Circus always likes to swing, and past the linden tree and the friendly, lazy drone of the honeybees getting nectar from its sweet-smelling flowers. A linden tree is the same as a basswood, and honeybees have the time of their lives when the clusters of creamy yellow flowers scatter their perfume all up and down the creek.

Going west from the tree, we followed a well-worn path toward the Sugar Creek bridge. Somewhere along that path, off to the left, we would probably find the tent. Old Man Paddler sometimes let people camp there for a few nights, or a week if they wanted to, under one of the spreading beech trees near the pawpaw bushes.

I kept my eyes peeled for the sight of a brown tent. As soon as we saw it, we would go bashfully up to it and ask if anybody had lost a billfold. Then we would have them describe it to us, and if it was like the one we had, we would give it to them. While we were there, we would get a closer look at the small-footed woman who had been wearing overalls last night and had been digging in the cemetery. There would probably be a car also, since there had been one last night.

But when we got to the bridge, there wasn't even a sign of a tent anywhere.

Poetry got an idea then. "Let's go down to the old sycamore tree and up through the cave to Old Man Paddler's cabin and ask *him*. He'll know where their camp is. They couldn't camp here anyway without his permission."

So away we went on across the north road and along the creek till we came to the sycamore tree, which, as you know, is at the edge of the swamp not far from the cave. Pretty soon we were all standing in front of the cave's big wooden door, which Old Man Paddler keeps unlocked when he is at home, because the cave is a shortcut to his cabin. The other end of the cave is the basement of his house.

Big Jim seized the white doorknob as different ones of us had done hundreds of times. In a jiffy we would be in the cave and on our way through the long, narrow passage to the cabin itself.

"Hey!" Big Jim exclaimed in a disappointed voice. "It's locked!"

I remembered that sometimes the old man kept the door closed and locked for quite a while when he was going to be away, or when he was on a vacation, or maybe when he was writing something or other and didn't want any company.

We turned and went back to the spring again and on up the creek in the other direction to see if we could find the tent we were looking for.

After walking and looking for maybe ten minutes without finding any tent, we came to another of Circus's favorite elm saplings near the rail fence that leads to Strawberry Hill. On the other side of the fence was Dragonfly's dad's pasture, where there were nearly always a dozen cows grazing.

While we were waiting for Circus to get up the tree and down again, I heard a rumbling noise a little like thunder mixed with the sound of wind blowing. I looked up quick to the southwest sky, expecting to see a rain cloud already formed and a storm getting itself ready to come pouring down upon us. But the big, yellow cumulus cloud was still where it had been. It did seem a lot bigger, and some other odd-shaped clouds had come from somewhere to hang themselves up there beside it to keep it company. Those other clouds probably carried a lot of their own rainwater to give to it so it would have enough to give our Sugar Creek farms a "real soaker," as Mom always called a big rain.

Then I looked over the rail fence into Dragonfly's dad's pasture and saw what looked like twenty scared cows racing furiously across the field. Their tails were up over their backs and switching fiercely as though the cows were terribly excited.

"It's a *stampede!*" Dragonfly cried.

Those cows acted blind and deaf and dumb and scared out of what few wits a cow has. They were all running wildly to get away from *something*—but I couldn't see anything for them to run away from.

Then I said, "I'll bet it's a lot of warble flies after them," remembering what Dad and I had been studying that week while we were looking up June beetles.

"What's a warble fly?" Little Tom Till wanted to know. His folks didn't have any cows. They always got the milk they drank at their house from Dragonfly's folks or mine.

Well, anybody who knows anything about a warble fly knows that it is a noisy, buzzing fly about half as big as a big black horsefly, and it lives only six days after it is born.

"A warble fly doesn't have any mouth and can't sting or bite a cow or anything," I said, feeling all of a sudden quite proud that I had learned so much about a lot of important things such as flies and beetles and other insects.

"Then why are cows scared of them?" Poetry asked. Even he didn't know that.

"They just make a fierce, buzzing sound and dive in and lay their eggs on the hair of the cows. Even as fast as the cows run, the warbles fly just that fast and flit in and out, laying eggs on them. Then, after six days of that kind of life, they die. They probably starve to death," I said, "not being able to eat."

"And cows are scared of an innocent egg?" Circus asked. But just then he seemed to get a little scared himself, as did all of us, because those twenty milk cows were making a beeline for our fence.

"They're coming for the shade," I said. "Warble flies don't like shade."

And I was right. In a cloud of whirling dust, those twenty cows came to an excited halt under the maple tree just over the fence from us. They didn't stay stopped but kept milling around, stamping their front feet, switching their tails madly, and doing the same kind of stamping with their back feet.

It seemed there were a lot of warble flies. I

saw and heard some of them diving in and out under the cows, which kept on switching their tails fiercely and stamping their feet. And that meant that if a boy had been there trying to milk one of them, he would have gotten the living daylights kicked out of him and his pail of milk spilled all over the ground or all over his clothes—and his parents would wonder what on earth had happened, if they saw him like that.

Not getting any peace, the excited cows, still pestered by the flies, started on another stampede. This time it was toward the bayou. And I knew that if they came to the weak place in the rail fence where we sometimes climbed over, they would dive through it and plow through the bushes and down the hill and right away would be in one of the sluggish ends of the bayou in the shade, which flies don't like. If the cows would stand up to their sides in the shady water, the warble flies would leave them alone, because warble flies always lay their eggs on the legs and underparts of a cow.

"Hey!" Dragonfly exclaimed excitedly, being as worried as his dad probably would have been. "They're going straight for the bayou!"

I knew if they did break through that fence and get into the water, they could also wade across and get into the cornfield on the other side, and they might eat themselves to death as cows sometimes do.

Dragonfly grabbed up a stick and started out after the cows as fast as his spindly legs could carry him, which wasn't too fast. Circus, who was faster, was already dashing fiercely down the other side of the fence to get to the place the cows were headed for.

I was running as fast as I could, following some of the gang and some of the gang following me, when I stepped into a brand-new groundhog den, which I had never seen before. Down I went *ker-plop* onto the ground. I was certainly surprised, because there hadn't been any hole there before. I knew every groundhog den there was for a mile in every direction from our house.

Then I noticed that the hole wasn't a groundhog den at all. It was another kind of hole. You could tell it hadn't been dug by any heavy-bodied, short-tailed, blunt-nosed, short-haired, short-legged, grizzly brown animal with four toes and a stubby thumb on its two front feet and five toes on its two hind feet—which is what a groundhog is. Besides, there wasn't any groundhog odor coming out of the hole, which my freckled nose was very close to right that second. And also there were the marks of a shovel and a woman's high-heeled shoes in the freshly dug soil.

7

I couldn't let myself stay there on the ground all sprawled out in five different directions, wondering what had happened to me. The gang had already gone and left me, running as fast as they could to catch up with and head off Dragonfly's dad's cows and keep them from breaking through the fence into the bayou. So I unscrambled myself, rolled over and up onto my feet, and soon was helping the gang by running and yelling and screaming to the cows to obey us—which they didn't.

Even as I ran, I was remembering what Dad and I had learned about warble flies—heel flies, some folks call them—and I thought, what if I was a real cow instead of merely being part of the time as awkward as one? If I were a cow and had my own brain knowing what it knew about warble flies, I would have the living daylights scared out of me.

Even though a warble fly doesn't have a mouth, so never eats, during the six days of its short life, it does lay eggs all over the legs and lower part of the cow. When a warble fly egg hatches, which it does in four or five days after it is laid, the thing that hatches out isn't a fly at all but a grub, which quick starts to bore its grubby way right through the cow's skin and into the cow. Once it gets inside, it starts on a chewing journey through the cow's inside, making its own path as it goes and making the cow itch like everything, which is maybe why some cows are not as friendly as other cows at certain times of the year.

I'll bet, if I were a cow, I wouldn't be worth a whoop to a farmer or anybody else who owned me, because I would probably feel the grub and maybe a half dozen or more of his grubby relatives working their way all through me, some of them stopping, as grubs do, right in my throat and staying a while just above where I would be chewing my cud.

During the whole five or six months a grub is inside a cow, it travels all around and finally chews a tunnel along the edges of the cow's spine until at last it stops and makes its home right under the skin of the back. There it chews a small hole through the cowhide so that it can breathe, which it does with its *tail*, getting good fresh country air through the hole and staying there nearly through the winter.

While still there, the grub develops into a wiggling, twisting, squirming warble. Finally it works its way out through its airhole and tumbles off to the ground. And if it is spring, and it doesn't get eaten up by a cowbird or a grackle or some other bird, it gets hard and black and finally changes into a fly. Then it makes a dive for the first cow it can find and starts to lay eggs as fast as it can before its six short days of noisy, buzzing life are over.

I was remembering all that as I galloped along after Dragonfly's dad's stampeding cows. I also remembered that in the wintertime in some parts of America, starlings and even magpies light on the backs of cows and start pecking away on them, trying to dig out the warbles with their sharp bills.

Well, if I were a cow and one of those high-voiced, buzzing flies was trying to lay her eggs on me, and I knew what would happen if it did, I would most certainly beat it for the shade, which warble flies don't like. Or if I could, I would find somebody's bayou or a little stream somewhere, splash myself out into it, and stand in the water up to my sides as I had seen cows do all around Sugar Creek for years without knowing before why they did it.

You should have seen Dragonfly's dad's cows ignore the few rails on the fence when they got to it. They broke right through without stopping and disappeared in a tail-swishing hurry into the brush. By the time we got to the fence ourselves, those cows were down in the sluggish water of the pond at the east end of the bayou.

Maybe I'd better tell you that Dad says American meat packers throw away enough grubby meat every year to have fed 83,000 people for a whole year—all because of the crazy warble flies. Also, Dad says a lot of cowhides have holes in them and people lose money that way too, because that part of the cow is where the leather is generally best—and what good is a piece of leather for making shoes or other leather goods if it has a hole in it? So a boy ought never to drive a bunch of cows out of a creek or a pond on a hot summer day but should let them stay there in the shade if they want to.

Cows don't give as much milk while they are worrying about noisy, whining flies either, and beef cattle don't get fat as fast. It's not easy to get fat if you worry a lot, which is maybe why some people are too thin.

Anyway, that is why we didn't get to look for the tent of the "turtledove" and the "bobwhite" until quite a while later. It took us almost an hour to get Dragonfly's dad's cows out of the bayou. We had to drive them out because the cornfield was on the other side, and you can't trust a cow with a cornfield any more than you can trust a boy or a girl with an open cookie jar.

If one of Dragonfly's dad's red heifers hadn't gotten a stubborn streak and decided she wanted to go on a wild run through the woods, we might not have found the tent for a long time. But while we were chasing her all around the brush and up and down the creek, she accidentally took us right to it.

"It was nice of that old red heifer to show us where the tent is, wasn't it?" Dragonfly said, after we had finally gotten her and the other cows back in Dragonfly's dad's dark cattle shed away from the flies. We were back again, not more than a hundred yards from the tent.

"Maybe the heifer smelled the calfskin in

the billfold in Bill's pocket, and it scared her. Maybe she thought Bill wanted to make a lot of billfolds out of her hide," Little Tom Till said, trying to be funny.

Circus said, "I don't think heifers think."

One of the first things we noticed about the camp when we got close to it was that they had picked one of the worst campsites in the whole woods. It was in the middle of the woods, half-way between our house and the spring, away back from the barefoot boys' path. So I couldn't have seen it when I had gone galloping to the spring a couple of hours ago. It was under one of the biggest, widest-spreading oak trees around there anywhere and would have shade all day, which would mean it wouldn't get a chance to dry out after a damp night. Nights often are damp in any territory where there is a river or a creek or a lake. And it wouldn't have any morning sun on it at all, as tents are supposed to have.

Any Scout knows that nobody should ever pitch a tent under an oak tree because the droppings from an oak will make the canvas rot quicker. Before you know it, you will have little holes scattered all over your roof, which will make it leak like everything when it rains.

Also, I noticed they had pitched the tent so that the flap would be open toward the *west*. Now, anybody who lives at Sugar Creek knows you shouldn't have the tent flap on the west side, because that is the direction most of our rains come from.

Besides, they would have to go too far to get their drinking and cooking water—clear down to the spring or else in the opposite direction to the Collins family's iron pitcher pump.

"They certainly don't know very much about camp life," Big Jim said, having been a Scout once. He had taught us all the different things about picking the best kind of campsite.

"It's a good thing they got a shovel," Tom Till said, seeing one standing against an iron-wood tree by their station wagon.

"Why?" Dragonfly said.

Little Tom Till answered, like a schoolboy who had studied his lesson and knew it by heart, "Because, where the tent's pitched now, if it rains, the water will run in from all sides and make a lake out of the floor."

Well, we brought it to a vote to see which one of us would go up and knock on the tent pole and ask if anybody had lost a billfold.

It took only a minute for me to win the election by a six-to-one vote—six for me and one against me, my vote being the one that was against.

So while the rest of the gang kept itself hidden behind some pawpaw bushes, I stepped out into the open and moseyed along as if I was only interested in seeing different things in the woods, such as a red squirrel in a tree or some kind of new beetle. Also I was walking carefully, so as not to awaken them if they were asleep, especially the one who was supposed to take an afternoon nap.

I forgot to tell you that the tent wasn't any ordinary brown canvas tent, either. It was *green* and was a sort of three-way tent, shaped like some of the ranch houses that people were building in our town. I could tell just by looking at the tent that it would be wonderful for a gang of boys to go camping in. One of the wings of the tent was only a canvas roof with the sides made out of some kind of netting to keep out different kinds of insects such as houseflies, deerflies, and blowflies. It could even keep out a horsefly or a warble fly if one wanted to get in. It would also keep out June beetles at night.

Right away I saw that somebody was resting on a cot inside one of the wings. I was too bashful to go any closer, because I could tell it was the woman herself lying there. She was maybe asleep, and it isn't polite to wake anybody out of a nap if you know she is taking one.

My heart was beating pretty fast because I was a little scared to do what I had been voted to do. But the man must have seen me or else heard all of us, because right then he opened the flap of the main part of the tent and came out with the forefinger of one hand up to his lips and the other hand making the kind of motions a person's hand makes when he wants you to keep still and not say a word.

I noticed that the brown-haired man was about as old as my reddish-haired dad and that he had a magazine in his hand as though he had been reading. He also motioned for me to stop where I was, which I did. He kept on coming toward me with his finger still up to his lips and shaking a warning finger with his other hand, which meant "*Shh*—don't say a word."

The man walked back with me to where the rest of the gang was behind the pawpaw bushes, and I noticed that he had a very nice face. Also he looked like an important city person, who might be extra smart and maybe had charge of a big office or maybe a store or something.

"Is there anything I can do for you boys?" he said in a very deep-sounding voice.

Even though he had a half-sad look in his eyes, I could tell he was a kind person and probably liked boys.

I looked at Big Jim, and he looked at me, and we all looked at different ones of us. Finally the rest of the gang's twelve eyes focused on my freckled face and red hair, so I looked up at the man and said, "Yes, sir. We found a billfold up along the creek—"

Little Tom Till cut in then, saying, "Little Jim here found it, and it's brown and has some dollar bills in it and three fives and one ten—"

"*Shh!*" Big Jim shushed him.

The man grinned, with a twinkle in his eyes, and I saw that the edge of one of his upper teeth had gold on it.

"That's all right. I can describe it for you," he said, which he did, giving all the details. "It has a tooled flying horse on the leather on the back, and the initials F. E., and the name Frances Everhard in the inside on the identification card. The license number of our car is 734-567. I was just ready to start looking for it."

There was something about the man that I liked, although I still thought there was an expression in his eyes that made it seem he was a little worried. I could tell he was the kind of man that would be nice to his wife, as Dad is to Mom. He might even be willing to do the dishes for her without being asked if she was extratired. I also noticed he kept looking at Little Jim as if he thought he was a very wonderful person.

"So you found it, did you, young man?" he asked.

"Yes, sir," Little Jim piped up in his mouse-like voice.

"Well, I want to thank you. I have a reward for you. If you boys come back later, say in about an hour, my wife will wish to thank you in person. She has some cookies that she bought on purpose for you, just in case you happened to visit us. She is having her nap now—doctor's orders are for her to sleep an hour every afternoon, you know."

We let the man have the billfold, which he took. Without opening it, he shoved it into his hip pocket. "Frances will be so thankful. I think she doesn't know she lost it yet. Maybe we won't tell her, eh?"

We promised *we* wouldn't, and he started to walk backward a little, which meant he was through visiting and we could go on home or somewhere.

Then, "Wait," Mr. Everhard said and stopped,

as we also did, because we had started off in our own direction. "How would one of you boys like to earn a quarter every day by bringing our drinking water from the spring or from up there at the Collins family house? One of you the Collins boy?"

I could feel myself blushing all over my freckled face, clear up to the roots of my red hair. I started to say yes, but Dragonfly beat me to it by saying, "He is," jerking his thumb in my direction.

The man came back to us, going on to explain. "This isn't the best place to pitch a tent —so far from a water supply. But somebody told us the spring was your gang's meeting place, so we decided to let you have your privacy."

Big Jim was pretty smart, I thought, when he spoke up politely and said, "That was very thoughtful of you." Then he added with a Big Jim grin, "You'll probably have more privacy yourself up here away from the noisy spring"— meaning us. Then he said, "Sure, we will be glad to bring your drinking water every day, won't we, Bill?"

"Sure," I said to Big Jim. "I'll even help you carry it."

The man was almost halfway back to his tent when he stopped and hurried back to us *again.* "Mr. Paddler has given us permission to dig a few holes around here in the woods," he said, "so don't be too surprised if you find a new one every now and then."

I started to say, "What are you digging them

for?" But I didn't because Big Jim scowled and shook his head at me.

A little later we stopped for a drink at the spring, and Circus said, "Old Man Paddler doesn't own the cemetery. Who would give them permission to dig out there in the cemetery at night? And why would they want to do it?"

"Maybe they're studying different kinds of soil. Maybe they have a lot of glass jars full of different kinds of dirt in the tent or in the station wagon," Poetry suggested.

"They wouldn't need to dig such deep holes just to get soil samples," Big Jim said, and I noticed he had a bit of a worried look on his face.

Poetry had another thought. "How are we going to spend our quarter every day—the one Bill is going to earn for us?" That wasn't funny.

Well, our mystery wasn't any nearer to being solved than it had been. One reason I felt quite disappointed was because I was sort of hoping that whoever had been digging in the cemetery the night before was what the police and detectives call a *ghoul*. That is a person who robs graves. And I was hoping that if it was such a person, maybe the gang could have a chance to help capture him or her.

We had done all we could that afternoon, although I was still wondering about the bobwhite whistle and the turtledove call. We talked that over while we were still at the spring and decided that maybe it was the way the man and his wife had of calling to each other—a sort of code such as we ourselves had. Whenever he wanted to call her, he could use the quail call, and she could answer it by cooing like a turtle-dove. If that was the meaning of it, it was kind of nice, and it showed that even married people could have fun together as my own mom and dad do a lot of times, in fact almost every day.

8

At the supper table at our house that night, I thought I'd never heard Mom and Dad laugh so hard. I was still thinking about the warble flies that had scared the living daylights out of Dragonfly's dad's cows. I told them all about it, crowding my words out between bites, and I was crowding the bites in too fast.

Dad said, "The heel flies are pretty bad this year. Nearly every farmer in Sugar Creek has been complaining about them. They were tormenting Old Brindle something fierce today. I didn't dare turn her out into the pasture without leaving the gate into the barnyard open so she could come rushing back in for the protection of the shade anytime she wants to."

"Speaking of cows," Mom said, and her voice lit up the way her face does when she has thought of something very interesting or funny. "I read something in a farm magazine today that was about the funniest thing I ever read."

"What was it?" Dad asked.

"Yes, what was it?" I said.

Dad and Mom were always reading things in magazines and telling them to each other, and I didn't always get in on their jokes. Sometimes I had to ask them what they were laughing about, and it didn't always seem as funny to me as it did to them. They also talked to each other about things that were not funny—things they had just that day learned about something in the Bible or something they had studied for next week's Sunday school lesson.

"I'll get it and read it for you," Mom said. She excused herself, left the table, went into the other room, and came back with a small magazine. "It's a ten-year-old schoolgirl's essay on a cow."

Even before she started reading it, I wasn't sure I was going to like it. I am close to being a ten-year-old boy myself, and I could imagine what a ten-year-old girl would write about a cow!

Dad cleared his throat as if he was going to read it himself or else so that he would be ready to laugh when the time came.

Mom started reading, while Charlotte Ann wiggled and twisted in her high chair. She was not interested in anybody's essay on a cow. All Charlotte Ann was interested in about cows was the milk she drank three times a day. So a story about a cow wouldn't be funny to her.

Even as I looked at Charlotte Ann, I was remembering that there were still plenty of unsolved things about our mystery. There was the picture of Charlotte Ann in the billfold; the strange-acting woman who dug holes in a graveyard at night and had permission to dig them all over the Sugar Creek territory, who had to rest every afternoon, and who went barefoot and waded in the riffles all by her-self—stuff like that.

Why did she have the picture of Charlotte Ann in her billfold? The very second Mom got through reading and she and Dad got through laughing, I would ask her about Charlotte Ann's picture.

Well, this is what Mom read, not getting to read more than a few lines before Dad inter-rupted her and the two of them started laugh-ing. Dad stopped her maybe a half-dozen times before she finished, and they laughed and laughed and kept on laughing, and Mom wiped her tears and held her sides, and Dad held his, and I grinned and scowled.

This is what Mom read:

The cow is a mammal. It has six sides—right, left, up and below, inside and outside. At the back is a tail on which hangs a brush. With this it sends the flies away so they don't fall into the milk. The head is for the purpose of growing horns and so the mouth can be somewhere. The horns are to butt with, and the mouth is to moo with. Under the cow hangs the milk. It is arranged for milking. When people milk, the milk comes, and there is never an end to the supply. How the cow does it I have never under-stood, but it makes more and more. The cow has a fine sense of smell. You can smell it far away. This is the reason for the fresh air in the country.

Well, that simply doubled up Mom and

Dad in laughter, and even Charlotte Ann pounded with her spoon on her ordinary wooden food tray, which I used to pound on years and years ago. It was probably the same spoon I had pounded with. She acted as if she was having the time of her life.

"What's the matter, Bill? Isn't it funny?"

"Not very," I said. "Anybody who is ten years old ought to know more about cows than that."

Right away Dad was ready to defend the girl by saying, "She was probably a city girl who didn't have any brothers," which also wasn't very funny.

"Say," I said to Mom, "have you had any new pictures taken of Charlotte Ann lately?"

"Why, no. Why do you ask?"

"You haven't had one taken of her sitting in that fancy high chair in the Sugar Creek Furniture Store?"

"No. Why do you ask?"

"Oh, I just wondered." I had made up my mind not to tell her any more.

As soon as supper was over, I started to do the dishes without being asked to for a change. I almost enjoyed it, because I was learning to enjoy doing things for Mom when she was tired. In fact, it makes me feel fine inside—almost as good as I feel when I am eating a piece of ripe watermelon—to do the dishes while she rests, because she is a pretty neat mom.

Dad was in the other room with her, talking to her while she rested. Mom was actually lying down while she was doing it, she was that tired.

"The most friendly couple is camping down in the woods," I heard her say. "They were here this afternoon a little while. She's the prettiest thing I think I ever saw. Kind of fancy, though, and wearing high-heeled shoes—not at all the kind an experienced camper or hiker would wear. They wanted a pail of well water, and I sold them a pound of Old Brindle's butter, which they are going to keep cool in the spring."

Hearing her say that, I sidled over to the kitchen door with Mom's apron on and the drying towel in my hands and listened to what else she was saying. I got there too late to get all of it.

"She's just out of the hospital, he told me. She doesn't look like there's a thing in the world wrong with her, but her husband—their name is Everhard—says she is under special treatment and she has been released to him. She's not at all dangerous, but she gets depressed at times, and sometimes right in the middle of the night she gets one of her spells."

I heard Dad sigh and say, "Being out here in the country with plenty of fresh air and good country food and with an understanding husband like that will be good for her. I wonder how long she has been that way."

Mom said, "He told me confidentially, when she was out in the car, that it started about a year ago. She's all right when she's all right, but these spells come on, and she cries. She never does anything desperate—only wants to go around digging holes in the ground."

That was as much as I got to hear right then because the phone rang. When Dad answered, it was Little Jim's mom, the pianist at the Sugar Creek church, wanting to talk to Mom about something or other.

Mom was always pleased when it was Little Jim's mom calling. Little Jim's mom was her best friend, and sometimes they talked and talked until one of them had to quit because she smelled something burning on the stove.

Well, I, the maid of the Collins family, went back to slosh my hands around a little longer in the hot sudsy water. Seeing our radio on the utility table and wondering what program was on, I wiped the water from my right hand and turned on the radio, dialing to a station that sometimes had a story for boys at that time. I tuned in just in time to hear the deep-voiced announcer in a terribly excited hurry say something about "those red dishpan hands," and then he galloped on to tell all the women listeners to be sure to use a certain kind of soap that would make their hands soft and pretty almost right away. The soap was also good for washing dishes.

Dad had to come through the kitchen on his way to the barn, so he stopped and listened with me. Then he said, "You using the right kind of soap, son?"

"I don't know. I hope so, but I'm afraid I am getting dishpan hands. Look at 'em!"

I held out my hands for him to look at, and he said with a mischievous grin in his voice, "Looks like you got dishpan hair too." Then he turned the radio down a little saying, "Your mother is resting, so keep it low."

"She's talking on the phone," I said.

"It's the same thing. You will find out she will be all full of pep when she gets through," which I knew might be the truth. Mom nearly always felt fine when she finished listening to and talking to Little Jim's mom, who was always cheerful on the telephone.

"She smiles with her voice," Mom always said about Little Jim's mom.

Dad went on out to the barn with the milk pail to see if the warble flies had tormented Old Brindle so much that day that she didn't have time to manufacture as much milk as usual, and I went on back to my half-cold dish-water.

I was just finishing washing the last dish and was getting ready to start drying them when Mom finished talking with and listening to Little Jim's mom. But when she came in, she was still tired. She sighed as she lifted the steaming teakettle and poured water over the dishes so she could dry them easier.

All of a sudden I got a half-sad, half-glad feeling in my heart, so I said to her, "You go on back in the other room and rest some more. I'm getting along fine." I suppose I was glad because for a change I actually wanted to help her, and maybe I was sad because Mom's sighs nearly always make me feel that way for some reason. She sighed again and started helping me. I decided to let her, because I didn't want to discourage her from helping a tired-out son with his work.

She was quiet for about three minutes, while all we could hear was the lazy ticking of the old clock on the mantel and the sound of the plates and cups and saucers and silverware. Pretty soon Mom said, still sadly, "I feel so sorry for her. Poor thing. If only she could believe and trust in God!"

I heard myself sigh the same kind of sigh Mom had sighed, and I felt sorry for the woman myself—knowing whom Mom meant.

Then I guess Mom decided that I ought to know more about Mrs. Everhard. But, first, she told me some things I never knew about the Collins family itself. Using a kind of sad voice, she said, "I want you to know before you get any older. It will help you to understand your mother and father better and all other people who have had to bury a little baby."

What? I thought, without saying a word.

Mom's voice sounded different from the way I had ever heard her talk as she went on. "Just two years before you were born, Bill, your father and I had to give back to God a very beautiful little three-weeks-old baby girl. She was so very lovely and sweet, and it broke our hearts, but we have tried to thank Him that He let us have her to love for even such a little while." She stopped, and again all I could hear was the lonely clock ticking so sadly that it seemed it must have felt sorry for Mom, too.

Still being very serious, she went on. "Then God gave us you to take her place, and you have been a great joy to us." Again she stopped.

I knew that if all her thoughts had come out in words, she could have added, "And also a lot of trouble." But Mom didn't, and I liked her even better, taking a sideways glance up at her out of the corner of my eye.

I guess maybe I had seen my mother's face a million times, but, while it's nearly always the same, I have never gotten tired of looking at it. She always looks just like my mom, even when she's all tired out or sad and hasn't had time to powder her nose from the hard work she is doing in the kitchen or out in the garden or orchard or somewhere.

She's a pretty wonderful mom, I thought and swallowed something in my throat, which stopped a couple of tears from getting into my eyes. Then I began working a little harder and faster on the dishes, which I had decided to help dry.

A little later Mom told me something else about the strange woman and her husband who were camping down in the Sugar Creek woods. It was something Little Jim's mom had just told her over the phone. Something had happened to the woman's mind. The doctors called it by some kind of fancy name that meant she was mentally ill and maybe would be for a while until she had time to get well again.

"Thousands of people get well from being mentally ill," Mom explained, "just like children do from such things as chicken pox and whooping cough. Sometimes, though, they have to have very special treatment in a special hospital.

"I can understand how she feels," she went on, "because, for a long time after we had buried little Nancy, it seemed she couldn't possibly be dead. She *had* to be alive, I kept thinking, and I kept imagining I could hear her crying in the other room."

"In there where Charlotte Ann is now?" I asked.

Mom didn't answer for a minute. She only nodded and sighed again. Then she said, "I never actually heard her voice, of course. And that is what is wrong with the dear little mother who is camping down there in the woods. You boys be very careful to be very kind and—"

"Is she an honest-to-goodness crazy woman?" I asked.

Mom replied, "Thoughtful people never say that anymore about a person who is ill in the way Mrs. Everhard is. They always say that they are *not well emotionally*. We try to understand them and to find out what made them that way. Sometimes, when they themselves come to understand what caused their illness, they begin to get well right away. In fact, some of them get well almost at once. Doctors try to give them something to hope for. It was only the grace of God and my believing in Him that spared me from going to pieces myself," she said. "He gave your father and me strength to stand the loss of your baby sister."

When Mom said "your sister," I did get a lump in my throat, because I was thinking, *What if it had been Charlotte Ann who had died?*

"You boys must not act surprised when you find those little freshly dug holes here and there in the woods or along the creek. When she gets one of her sad spells, she imagines her baby is still alive, even though it was buried, and she starts digging holes in the woods or along the creek, looking for it. She thinks it was buried alive when she feels like that. She will dig awhile and then stop to listen to see if she can hear it crying."

When Mom said that, I remembered that we had seen her do that very thing in the old cemetery last night.

"Can't the doctors make her well?" I asked Mom.

"Not with just medicine alone. One thing the doctor has prescribed for her is that she attend some church regularly—a church where the minister believes and preaches the Bible and what it teaches about heaven and the wonderful place it is, and how people can meet their loved ones there, alive and well—all through trusting in the Savior. The doctor thinks that if Mrs. Everhard can learn to trust in God and to believe that she will see her baby again, she will be cured."

9

Well, it seemed after that wonderful talk with Mom that I, Bill Collins, was going to be a better boy than I had ever been in my life before—although I didn't see how I could change all of me so quick. Anyway, now I thought I knew why Mom every now and then sighed even when I couldn't see a thing to sigh about. Maybe a sad thought came to her that wasn't caused by the hot weather or from being tired or because I might have been a bad boy, which I sometimes used to be.

Several weeks went by during which the gang found maybe twenty-five different-sized holes in different places in the woods and along the creek. Also we were not surprised when most anytime we heard a quail call and a turtledove answer it. Sometimes, though, it was the woman who gave the quail call, and the man was the turtledove who answered.

It began to be almost fun to hear them, because we could tell that they liked each other a lot. They were kind of like a gang themselves, except that there were only two of them. And their whistling to each other was like a game of some kind, just as we ourselves played different kinds of games. It was like having a secret code. They wanted us all to stop at their green tent every day, and nearly always Mrs. Everhard had something for us to eat, which made it easy to remember to stop. Of course, I had to go anyway to carry water from our iron pitcher pump to them.

Each Sunday the Everhards came to our church to hear our minister, who in nearly every sermon mentioned something about heaven and how to get there—such as if you know that you are an honest-to-goodness sinner and that you can't save yourself, which nobody can, and if you trust the Savior Himself to forgive all your sins, you will be sure to go there. He said that all the babies that ever died are already there, because the blood of Jesus Christ shed upon the cross took care of all of them—and things like that.

I had to watch myself to keep from looking across the church all the time to watch Mrs. Everhard and see if she was believing the sermon. The only thing was, instead of looking at the minister, she kept looking at Mom or Dad or me, whichever one of us was holding Charlotte Ann, as if she wondered if we were taking care of her right.

One Sunday, right in the middle of the sermon, she quickly stood and walked down the aisle in a hurry to the outside door, her husband after her. A little later I heard through the open window the station wagon engine start, and I knew he was taking her back to the tent. Maybe she left so that she wouldn't cry in church.

That afternoon when Dad was helping our minister and some other men hold a jail meeting and Mom and I were alone, Mr. Everhard came over to our house to borrow Charlotte Ann a while.

"*Borrow* her!" Mom said with an astonished voice and face.

He answered, "Yes, Charlotte Ann looks so very much like our own little Elsa used to look that I thought if Frances could hold her a while, and listen to her as she pretends to talk, it might make her feel better. She's very much down today."

Well, I had heard of people borrowing nearly everything else. Around Sugar Creek the gang's different mothers borrowed different kinds of kitchen things, which they sometimes ran out of and had to have in a hurry—as fast as a boy could run to the neighbor's and get it. Sometimes Dragonfly's dad borrowed our brace and bit or hand drill or keyhole saw, and Dad would sometimes borrow them back again if he needed them in a hurry—I getting to run to Dragonfly's house to get them but not getting to stay and play with Dragonfly, which made it a very hard errand to be sent on. Also different members of the gang would borrow knives or fishhooks or bobbers or other things from each other.

But whoever heard of anybody borrowing a baby?

I could see Mom wasn't going to like the idea. And if she didn't, I wasn't going to, either.

But I guess that because she felt so sorry for the lady, and wanted her to get well fast, she quickly thought up a way to say yes and not hurt Mr. Everhard's feelings or her own.

"If you will borrow me too, that will be fine," she said cheerfully, and he answered, "Certainly. It will soon be time for afternoon tea anyway."

"What about *me?*" I said, all of a sudden trying to be funny and probably not being very. "Anybody want to borrow a good-looking, red-haired, homely faced boy?" I didn't really want to go, though, because some of the gang might come over to play.

But Mom said quickly, "Certainly, son, come right along."

And so it turned out that I went with Mom and Charlotte Ann and Mr. Everhard, carrying a gallon thermos jug of cold water to earn my twenty-five cents for that day.

The first thing I noticed when we came to within a few yards of the green ranch-style tent was that the wing with the mosquito netting sidewalls had in it a baby's playpen. In the pen were a lot of things for a baby girl to enjoy—a doll, a pink teddy bear, a very small broom like the one Charlotte Ann helps Mom sweep with, and a little tea set for playing house. Beside the tent, hanging by a rope and a spring, was a jumper swing like the one that used to hang from the limb under the plum tree in our yard, where Charlotte Ann used to sit and bounce herself up and down and laugh and gurgle and have the time of her life. Now it's too little for her.

"The poor, dear girl," Mom said under her breath with a sigh and in my direction. Mr. Everhard had gone on into the tent to tell his wife she had company, and Mom was looking at the baby things with a sort of faraway expression in her eyes.

I could hear voices inside the tent, and it sounded for a minute as if there was a half-argument. Then the canvas flap of the tent opened, and Mrs. Everhard came out.

Mom gasped when she saw her, because of the way she was dressed and what she had in her hand.

"Such a pretty dress," Mom said, half to me and half to nobody.

I hardly ever paid any attention to what anybody was wearing, especially a woman or a girl, because it didn't seem important. But I guess any woman or maybe even a boy would gasp at the green and brown and yellow and red summery-looking dress Mrs. Everhard had on. It had a lot of milkweed flowers on it and pretty swallowtail butterflies with spread wings on each flower. Her yellowish hair was the same color as the sulfur butterflies that fly around our cabbage plants with the white ones, and I noticed it was still combed the way it had been in church, with some kind of sparkling pin in it. She was wearing a pair of dark glasses and green and yellow shoes.

To my tangled-up surprise, she had in her

hands a shovel like the one she had been using to dig in the cemetery. She looked all around in a sort of dazed circle, not seeing us at first, then she started off in a hurry in the direction of Strawberry Hill.

Quick as anything and without knowing I was going to do it, I whistled a sharp bobwhite whistle that flew as straight as an arrow right toward her. It made her stop stock-still and turn and stare. Then her eyes fell on Charlotte Ann, whom Mom had dressed especially for the visit in a little blue organdy playsuit that made her look as cute as a bug's ear and even cuter.

Mrs. Everhard dropped her shovel as if it had a hot handle and gasped an excited gasp the way women who like babies do when they see a pretty one. She said, "You *darling* baby!" She started to make a beeline for her, as though she was going to pick her up, then she whirled around fast and disappeared into the tent.

For just a second I had a queer fluttering feeling in my heart. It was kind of as if fifty pretty black-and-yellow swallowtail butterflies had been fluttering in front of my eyes in the bright sunlight and then all of a sudden had flown toward the green tent and disappeared all at once. It was the same kind of happy feeling I get when I hear a wood thrush singing but can't see it and wish I could.

A minute later she was back outside again with a camera. For a while she acted as if nobody was around except Charlotte Ann. Her extra-pretty face was all lit up, and she seemed very happy.

"She looks enough like my own Elsa to be a twin," she told Mom. "In fact, almost enough to *be* her." Then she sighed a heavy sigh, and so did Mom.

Well, we had a very interesting visit that afternoon at the ranch-house tent. As soon as Charlotte Ann got over being bashful, she let Mrs. Everhard hold her and take all kinds of pictures of her: in the playpen, in the jumper swing, lying on a blanket, and doing different other things. She had her bobwhite husband take a picture of the two of them while she held Charlotte Ann on her lap.

Everybody had a good time except me. I like to keep my mind in a boy's world, and nobody could do that when there were three grown-ups and a baby around. So I asked if they would like me to get some fresh, cold water from the spring. When they said yes, I took a thermos jug and shot like a redheaded arrow out past the pawpaw bushes toward the old overhanging linden tree above the spring.

I was thinking as I ran that the mystery of the little holes being dug all over Sugar Creek territory was all explained now, and it looked as if the gang would have to scout around for some other problem to set our seven different kinds of brains to working on.

I didn't know that because Charlotte Ann

and the woman's dead baby looked so much alike, I was going to have to put my own brain to work in a very special way before the summer was over. And I guess I never realized just how wonderful a person I had for a baby sister until I thought I was going to lose her. As quick as I can, I will start telling you all about it.

First, though, I have to tell you something else about Charlotte Ann, because some of the people who will read this story don't know much about her, and it will help them understand how come she got lost.

At our house, we always had more fun than you can shake a stick at, taking care of Charlotte Ann, in spite of the times when she was a nuisance. Dad especially had a lot of fun because he nearly always had to put her to bed at night after she was a little bigger than a little baby. When she got to be about two years old, going to bed was one of the things Charlotte Ann didn't like even more than she didn't like anything else. Before that, we didn't have to worry about her getting all the sleep she needed, because she would go to sleep anywhere, anyplace, and nearly anytime. But all of a sudden she was a two-year-old and seemed to have ideas of her own about such things as going to bed at night and taking afternoon naps.

"That is because at two," Mom said, after reading a book on how to take care of babies at that age, "they are great imitators. Whatever they see you do, *they* want to do, too. They like to do grown-up things before they are old enough, or strong enough, or have sense enough to."

"Or sense enough *not* to," Dad said, and Mom agreed with him, both of them seeming to think that was funny. But I couldn't understand what they meant.

"Also," Mom said, "a two-year-old has to have twelve hours of sleep at night and at least one hour in the afternoon every day." She was talking to me at the time. "You had to have it when you were a baby, and we saw to it that you got it whether you wanted it or not—which you generally didn't. And see what a wonderfully fine strong boy it made out of you."

I got a mischievous streak when she said that and answered, "I can see how maybe I am a wonderful boy and very fine, but I feel very *weak* right now." Just a minute before that, she had ordered me to carry in a couple of armfuls of wood for the wood box, which never seemed to have sense enough to stay full and always managed to get itself empty at the very time I didn't want to fill it and generally when I wanted to do something else.

"See," I said to Mom, "before you asked me to get that wood, I could swing both arms up over my head and still feel fine just like this." I held my arms over my head as if I was as strong as the imaginary man Atlas, who used to hold the world on his shoulders. "But now," I went on, "I'm so weak I can't lift my right arm more than this high, just about as high as my waist."

I had heard Little Jim's dad do that with his

mom once. It had sounded cute, so I had decided to try it on my parents the first chance I got.

Mom, who was getting dinner at the time, stopped stirring the gravy, turned, looked through the lower part of her glasses at me, and said, "Poor boy. That's too bad. If you can't lift your hand any higher than your waist, then how can you carry in the wood? I'll take care of the wood myself. Maybe you'd better go and lie down for an hour while your father and I have dinner, because, your mouth being a little higher than your waist, you won't be able to feed yourself."

For some reason I right away went out and carried in several loads of wood without saying another word, getting it done about the same time Mom had dinner ready.

But let me get back to telling you about Charlotte Ann and how she got mixed up in our mystery. The worst trouble we had with her was that when we finally got her into bed at night or in the afternoon when it was her nap time, she didn't want to go to sleep. Sometimes she would call for a drink of water or something to eat, and sometimes she would come toddling out in her bare feet to wherever Mom and Dad and I were and interrupt our reading or our talking or Dad's evening nap on the davenport. She nearly always came out wide awake, acting very friendly and as if she felt more at home when she was up than when she was down.

"What on earth makes her want to do that?" I said one day. "Doesn't she have sense enough to stay in bed?"

"She's lonesome," Mom answered. "She's lonesome, and she has to have lots of attention. You were that way when you were little."

"Oh, quit telling me about when I was little years and years ago," I said, not wanting to even be reminded that I ever had been a baby.

As I started to say, getting Charlotte Ann to bed was a hard problem. And when Dad had to be away, it got to be my job to help Mom make her go.

But when Mom and Dad were both away, then I had to do it all by myself—being the baby-sitter.

One very hot afternoon, Mom and Dad both had to be gone for two or three hours, and so they let me stay home to take care of Charlotte Ann. They gave me orders to see to it that she took her afternoon nap between 1:30 and 2:30, or as near to that as I could get her to. And if it rained, I was to close all the windows—things like that.

"Take good care of her," Mom said, as she looked out the car door window, all dressed up in her Sunday dress.

"I will," I promised, and she and Dad went spinning out through the front gate, past "Theodore Collins" on the mailbox, and onto the highway. Their car stirred up a big cloud of white dust that moved slowly off in the direction of Bumblebee Hill and the old cemetery.

10

I shut the gate after Mom and Dad, and Charlotte Ann and I went hand in hand toward the house to take her nap. That is, her hand was in mine. She didn't want it to be there because she knew it was nap time, and she didn't want to take one.

"It's not hard to take a nap," I said to her. "You just lie down and shut your eyes, and that's all there is to it. I'm the baby-sitter, and you are the baby-lying-downer. My first job is to get you to bed, so here we go."

I was using a very cheerful voice, but she seemed to be suspicious of such a voice coming from me. Besides, she was still a little tearful from Mom and Dad's having gone and leaving her at home with me.

I realized that I was going to have to use one of Dad's tricks to get her to want to go to bed, one he used sometimes at night. I had seen him put her to bed maybe a hundred times, so I looked down at her and said cheerfully, "OK, kid. Let's get going."

I was surprised at how easy it was at first. It didn't take long to get her ready because Mom had said she could rest in her playsuit, which Mom called her sunsuit. Just as Dad does, I pretended to be a poor, crippled, old grandfather, saying to her with a trembling voice as if I was suffering terribly, "I've got to get into that other room, and I need somebody to help me walk."

I started limping badly toward the room where she was supposed to sleep, going very slowly like a very crippled old man, staggering and limping and whining and complaining.

If there is anybody Charlotte Ann likes better than anybody else, it is Old Man Paddler. She must have imagined that I was Mr. Paddler, because quick as anything she made a dive in my direction, clasped her small hands around my right knee and held on tight while I limped the best I could with one leg and walked the best I could with the other. We struggled toward the room where her small bed was. All the way there, I kept on complaining with a trembling voice, saying, "Poor old man. How can I walk without a nice little girl to help me?"

The very minute we got to her bed—the green window shade was down, and it was almost dark—she decided to do as she does at night when she says her prayers before getting into bed. Right away she was down on her knees and making me get down beside her. I bent my poor, old rheumatic knees down to the hard floor.

Without waiting for me to say anything, she started in her babyish voice trying to say the prayer Dad had been teaching her:

"Now I lay me down to sleep.
  I pray Thee, Lord, my soul to keep.
  If I should die before I wake,
  I pray Thee, Lord, my soul to take.
      For Jesus' sake. Amen."

It was the same prayer I used to say myself years and years ago. Sometimes even yet when I kneel down to say a good-night prayer to God and I am very tired and sleepy, before I know it I am saying it myself even though I am too big to say just a little poem prayer.

As soon as her prayer was finished, I swooped her up and flip-flopped her into bed, but for some reason or other she was as wide awake as anything. She didn't stay lying down but sat straight up in bed with a mischievous grin all over her cute face. She was the most wide-awake baby I ever saw.

"I want my dolly," she ordered me in her own language, which is what she always does at night.

"OK," I said and got it for her from the other room, where I found it upside down and lying on its face. I handed it to her.

"I want my rag dolly too," she said.

"OK, I'll get your dirty-faced rag dolly." I went to the corner of the room, where it was lying on its side with its left foot stuck in its face. I carried it to her and tossed it into the bed with her, where it socked her in the cheek but didn't hurt. Then I said, "OK, now. Go to sleep."

I was halfway to the door when she called again, saying, "I want my 'puh'"—meaning her little pink doll pillow.

I came back and sighed down hard at her, then started looking everywhere for her pink pillow, wondering what else she would want and why. I soon found out because next she wanted her hanky, a pretty colored handkerchief that Dad had had to get for her every night all summer and which she always held close to her face when she went to sleep, since it was very soft. Mom said, "She likes to feel secure, and all these things help her to feel that way. She imagines the dollies are honest-to-goodness people, and she feels she isn't alone when they are with her in bed. They keep her from being afraid."

I couldn't help but think that Poetry—who is always quoting a poem—if he were here, would probably quote one by Robert Louis Stevenson, which goes like this:

> In winter I get up at night
> And dress by yellow candlelight.
> In summer quite the other way
> I have to go to bed by day.

For some reason or other as I looked down at her cuddling her dollies, I had never liked her so well in my whole life—even though I was still half disgusted with her for making me bring her so many things. I guess I was also a little worried too, which probably helped me to like her better. I kept thinking about the woman who had been digging holes in the earth, the one who thought Charlotte Ann looked enough like her own dead Elsa to be her twin—in fact, enough like her to *be* her. I wished the woman would hurry up and get well, but she didn't seem to be improving very much, because the gang had kept on finding new holes all around Sugar Creek.

Pretty soon Charlotte Ann's eyes went shut and stayed shut, and her regular breathing showed that she was asleep.

Realizing that at last she was asleep, I went out through the living room into the kitchen and through that. Out of doors, I closed the screen door more quietly than it had been closed for a long time and went on out toward the iron pitcher pump—suddenly being very thirsty.

Halfway to the pump I stopped on the board walk and turned around to see if anything was wrong. I felt that something was. Nearly always by the time I got that far out of doors, I heard the screen door slam behind me. This time it hadn't done it, and it was a bit confusing to me not to hear it.

Baby-sitting was hard work, I thought, and it would be silly to do two long hours of it actually sitting down.

A few minutes later I was up on our grape arbor in a perfect position for eating a piece of pie upside down. But I didn't have any pie, so I couldn't baby-sit that way.

Pretty soon I was tired of being up on that narrow two-by-four, so I wriggled myself down and walked over to the water tank on the other side of the pump where a lot of yellow butterflies, seeing me come, made a scramble in different fluttering directions. Then right away the air was quiet again as they settled themselves down all around the edge of a little water puddle.

Maybe I could get Dad's insect book and look up a new insect for him. Maybe I could look up something about yellow butterflies, which laid their eggs on Mom's cabbage plants, and also the green larvae, which hatched out and ate the cabbages. But I wasn't interested in getting any more education just then.

When I spied my personally owned hoe leaning against the toolhouse on the other side of the grape arbor, an idea popped into my head to do a few minutes' baby-sitting by hoeing a couple rows of potatoes in the garden just below the pignut trees near which Dad had buried Old Addie's two red-haired pigs. But for some reason or other I began to feel very tired, and I could tell it would be very boring to baby-sit that way.

I moseyed along out to where Old Addie was doing her own baby-sitting near a big puddle beside her apartment house, lying in some straw that was still clean. She was acting very lazy and sleepy and grunting while her six red-haired, lively youngsters were having a noisy afternoon lunch.

"Pretty soft," I said down to her, but she didn't act as if she even recognized me.

I remembered a silly little rhyme, which I had heard in school when I was in first grade:

Six little pigs in the straw with their
   mother,
Bright-eyed, curly-tailed, tumbling on
   each other.
Bring them apples from the orchard
   trees,
And hear those piggies say, "Please,
   please, please."

That gave me an idea. I scrambled out to the orchard, picked up six apples, and brought them back. Leaning over the fence, I called out, "Here, piggy, piggy, piggy. Here are some nice apples. Say please, and you can have them."

But they ignored me, not only not saying please but probably not even saying thank you in pig language to their mother.

So I tossed my six apples over into the hog lot, where they rolled up to the open door of Addie's apartment. And that was the end of her six babies' afternoon lunch. She shuffled her heavy body to her feet, swung it around, and started in on those apples as though she was terribly hungry.

Well, what next? I thought. I wondered if old Bentcomb, my favorite white hen, who always laid her egg in the nest up in our haymow, had laid her egg yet today. It was too early to gather the eggs, but I could get hers if she had it ready.

Into the barn and up the ladder I went, and there she was with her pretty white neck and head. Her long, red bent comb hung down over her right eye like a lock of brown hair drops down over the right eye of one of Circus's many sisters, who, even though she is ordinary-looking, doesn't act as though she thinks I am a dumbbell, the way some girls do that go to the Sugar Creek School.

"Hi, old Bentcomb," I said, but she ducked her head and ignored me.

"Pretty soft life," I said. "You don't have to worry about taking care of a baby sister while your parents are away."

Down the ladder I went and shuffled back across the barnyard, thinking maybe it would be a good idea to peek in under the window shade to see if Charlotte Ann was still asleep.

11

As I told you, it was one of those terribly hot afternoons. The Collins family had been hoping for a week that it would rain, because our crops needed a real soaker. Just to find out for sure if it was going to, I lifted up a little wooden step at the door on the north side of our house to see if a smooth, round stone that was half buried there was wet. It always is when it is going to rain. Dad looks there himself when he wants to find out whether it will rain. Mom teases him about it.

The minute the daylight streamed into where the dark had been under that step, a lot of different kinds of bugs scrambled for a place to hide. I noticed especially a big, black cricket, maybe the very one that sings every night just outside Mom's and Dad's bedroom window, which Mom says sings her to sleep. She likes to hear crickets but isn't interested in looking at them or touching them.

The smooth, round stone was wet, I noticed, which meant that there was a lot of humidity in the air. Then I put the step back down again and went to the corner of the house to see if there was a big yellowish cloud in the southwest, and there was. So it might rain before night, I thought.

Just that second I saw a large, tiger-colored swallowtail butterfly out by the orchard fence, fluttering around a red thistle blossom. Because the swallowtail is one of the largest butterflies in our whole territory, I knew Dad would be especially pleased if I could catch one for our collection. So I quickly circled the house to the toolshed, scooped up Dad's butterfly net, and a minute later was out by the orchard fence where one of the most beautiful butterflies I had ever seen was acting as if the nectar of that big bull thistle blossom was about the sweetest thing in the world to eat.

Generally we didn't allow any bull thistles to grow on our farm. But because Dad knew that swallowtail butterflies like milkweed and thistle flowers better than any others, we had let this one grow, hoping a swallowtail would decide to live around our place. One of the prettiest sights a boy ever sees on a farm is a beautiful butterfly drifting around and lighting on the flowers, its different-colored wings folding and unfolding and making a boy feel all glad inside.

The swallowtail was on the other side of the woven wire fence, which was very hard to climb over, so I hurried to the orchard gate near the cherry tree. I got to the thistle just as the gorgeous yellow and black swallowtail decided to leave, floating lazily along like a feather in the wind, with me right after it, swinging my net and missing it and running and getting hot and still not catching it.

Then all of a sudden I heard a quail's whistle. I stopped and looked all around, expecting to see either Mr. Everhard or his wife. A second later I saw which one it was, and it was Mr. Everhard. I wanted to give a mournful turtledove call to answer him, but instead I listened for his wife to answer. But she didn't.

Seeing me, he called, "Have you seen anything of Mrs. Everhard?"

"No, I haven't," I called back, deciding to forget about the swallowtail I was after. Besides, when I had taken my eye off the butterfly, I had lost it.

"She was taking her afternoon nap," Mr. Everhard said, "so I went to the creek a while, but when I came back she was gone. You sure she's not up at your house?"

"I'm sure," I said, suddenly remembering that it had been a long time since I was inside our house. Also, for some reason I decided I had better go quick to see if Charlotte Ann was still asleep or if she had waked up and maybe had gone somewhere herself.

"Let's go look," I said to Mr. Everhard and started to run fast, with him right after me.

All the way through the orchard to the big bull thistle and the gate, not bothering to wait for Mr. Everhard, I was thinking over and over, *Mrs. Everhard had been taking a nap while her husband was away, and when he came back she was gone, and he couldn't find her—gone, and he couldn't find her. And she was crazy—no, emotionally ill—*

and our Charlotte Ann looked enough like her dead baby, Elsa, to be her twin. Enough like her to be her.

I tried to run faster and couldn't. Instead of flying along like a bird in a hurry, I felt that I was just crawling like a swallowtail butterfly's reddish-brown larva crawling along a parsnip leaf in our garden, which is the kind of leaf a swallowtail's larva likes to eat best.

Hurry! Hurry! Hurry! If ever I hurried, I hurried then.

I darted past the big red thistle blossom, not even stopping to glance at it to see if there might be another swallowtail fluttering around it. I darted through the still-open gate and past the front doorstep, around the house, past the grape arbor to the back screen, which I remembered now I hadn't locked from the outside as I should have.

She's got to be there, I thought. Why, she could have toddled out that door and gone to the barn or even through the front gate and across the dusty road and through the woods to the spring and the creek, *and she doesn't know how to swim!*

She didn't know how to swim!

Then I thought, what if Mrs. Everhard had gotten one of her spells and decided that Charlotte Ann really *was* her baby and had come to get her and had run away with her—*kidnapped her?* She *had* to be there in her crib asleep—*had* to be!

I made a barefoot dash through the kitchen and the living room and into the dark bedroom, not being able to see in the almost dark because I had been out in the bright sunlight and my eyes were not adjusted yet. I ran to her bed.

"Charlotte Ann," I exclaimed, "are you here?" and I thrust my hands down into her crib to see if she was.

Then I got the most terrible feeling I'd had in my life. I just felt terrible. *Awful!* A million worried thoughts went whirling around in my mind, for *Charlotte Ann wasn't there. She was gone!*

Gone! Gone away somewhere, and I didn't know where.

Just then I heard a heavy rumbling noise outside the house like the noise a wagon makes going across the Sugar Creek bridge. It also sounded a little like a powerful car starting. But, of course, it couldn't be that, because any car outside wouldn't be just starting; it would be stopping instead.

Charlotte Ann wasn't in her crib. I hurried out of the room, calling her name and looking in every other room in the house, upstairs and down and up again, calling and looking frantically. She *had* to be in the house. *Had* to be!

But she wasn't. I dashed back downstairs and out through the back screen door just as Mr. Everhard got there. He didn't act as worried as I felt, but the fleeting glimpse I got of his face when I told him, "There's nobody here," didn't make me feel any better.

Then I heard the rumbling again. It was louder and closer. I looked up toward the sky, and the sound had come from a big black cloud in the southwest over the tops of the pignut trees. And without having to look under the wooden step at our front door, I knew it was going to rain. It was going to rain a real soaker. I could tell by the way a lot of angry-looking clouds were churning around up there that there would be wind too, and that meant every window in the house and every door ought to be shut tight. But with Charlotte Ann on my mind, I didn't have time to do it.

"Help me look for Charlotte Ann," I yelled back over my shoulder to Mr. Everhard as I darted across the barnyard toward Old Red Addie's apartment house, calling Charlotte Ann's name and looking for a shock of pretty reddish-black curls and an aqua-colored sunsuit.

The word "aqua," which I knew meant "water," didn't help me feel any better. Neither did the word "sunsuit," because the sun was already hidden by clouds, and the wind, which nearly always rushes ahead of a storm to let you know one is coming, was already making a wild noise in the leaves of the trees in the orchard and the woods.

Just then there was a banging sound on the west side of the house, and Mom's big washtub, which she always keeps there on a wooden frame to catch the rainwater, went *bangety-plop-sizzle* across the slanting cellar door and the board walk and out across the yard, where it struck the plum tree, glanced off, and went on, landing *ker-wham* against the walnut tree.

Clouds of dust, whipped up by the wind, came from the direction of the pignut trees, which were being tossed around wildly.

I knew we were not only in for a real soaker but a lot of dangerous wind. The whole sky was already cloud-covered except for the northeast corner, which is above Strawberry Hill and the cemetery.

Charlotte Ann wasn't in the barn, and neither was Mr. Everhard's pretty wife.

My conscience was screaming at me for being such a careless baby-sitter as to leave a two-year-old baby girl alone in the house and also for not locking the doors when I did leave the house.

Being a boy who believes in God, and also knowing that "heaven helps them that help themselves," as Dad had told me, some of the stormy thoughts that were whirligigging in my mind were all mixed up with worried prayers and wondering what my parents would think with their baby lost in the storm.

Charlotte Ann, being a two-year-old and a "great imitator," having seen me rushing out our back door and across the lawn, through the gate, and past "Theodore Collins" on our mailbox, probably had done that herself. By this time she could be through the rail fence on the other side of the road and toddling along as fast as a two-year-old can toddle, getting up and falling down and getting up again. She was probably away down in the woods and maybe had already gotten to the spring and the creek—and you know what could have happened to her.

Just then the wind swept off my straw hat and sent it on a high, wild flight out across the yard, straight toward the walnut tree, where it swished between the two ropes of the rope swing, went on and landed in the dusty road, was picked up again by the wind, and was whipped out toward the rail fence itself in the direction of Strawberry Hill and the old cemetery.

I was wishing my parents were there to help me. I was also glad they weren't there, because it would be time soon enough for Mom to start worrying. And once Mom gets started worrying, it's hard for her to stop unless she takes a minute to quickly read or remember a Bible verse, and then that verse is just like a new broom—it sweeps the worry clear out of her mind, she says.

The most important thing in the world right then was to find Charlotte Ann and not let her get caught in what I could tell was the beginning of a terrific storm. I was having a hard time to stay on my feet myself, and I knew a wind like that would blow Charlotte Ann over as easily as anything. Of course, when a baby falls down, it generally doesn't hurt much because a baby doesn't have as far to fall as a grown-up person. But a wind like this one could not only blow her off her feet but could slam her against a tree or a rail fence or into the briers of a rosebush. Or if she was anywhere near the creek, it might actually blow her into it.

So, scared half to death, I yelled to Mr. Everhard, "Come on! We've got to find them!"

And he snapped into the fastest life I had ever seen a dignified man snap into. Both of us right away were hurrying past "Theodore Collins" on our mailbox, and soon we were out in the woods.

"If they are anywhere near the tent or the station wagon, they will probably go there to get out of the rain," he said. "Let's go back to camp first."

Before he finished gasping out the last word of what he had started to say, we were already on the way.

We both hoped that they were not in the tent, though, because the wind might blow the tent over. If they had gotten into the station wagon, it would be a lot better. Mr. Everhard was yelling that to me above the roar of the storm as we raced along, dodging the trees and bushes and leaping over fallen logs. It seemed we'd never get there.

In fact, it seemed it had never taken me so long in my whole life to get to that part of the woods. Then I felt a splatter of rain on my hand and another on my face, and in seconds it was just like a whole skyful of water was falling. The rain was coming down the way it does when Mom says it's coming down in sheets. In fact, it started coming down so hard that I couldn't see where I was going. The rain in my face and eyes and on my bare red head kept me straining to see anything.

It must have taken us almost fifteen minutes —which seemed an hour—to get to the tent. It was still standing, but not all of it. The wing that had had the netting sidewalls was all squashed in. A big dead branch from the oak tree under which the tent had been pitched— and shouldn't have been—had fallen on it, smashing the playpen and other things in that little room. The rest of the tent was only half standing.

For a minute, I imagined Charlotte Ann and Mrs. Everhard in there somewhere, the big branch having fallen on them. They might be terribly hurt or even worse. They might not even be alive.

Beside me I could hear Mr. Everhard saying something, and it sounded like a prayer. I couldn't hear him very well, but I caught just enough of the words: "O dear God, please spare her life. Spare her, and I'll be a better man. I'll do right. I'll—I'll give my heart to You and be a Christian."

Even as I stumbled blindly along with him the last few yards to the twisted-up tent, I couldn't help but think what I had heard our minister say lots of times—that even a kind man could still not be an honest-to-goodness Christian. Mr. Everhard might never have given his heart to the Lord Jesus and had his sins forgiven, I thought.

I also couldn't help but think how neat it would be if Mr. and Mrs. Everhard *would* honest-to-goodness for sure give their hearts to God and be saved and say so some Sunday morning in the Sugar Creek church as other people did almost every month.

Well, it took us about half a minute to get the rest of the way there in that blinding rainstorm. We looked inside the part of the tent that was still standing and saw that neither Charlotte Ann nor Frances Everhard was there.

As glad as I was that the dead branch hadn't fallen on them, I still didn't feel much relieved. I knew that they were somewhere else; and if they weren't in the station wagon, they were still out in the dangerous storm, and nobody knew where. I also thought that if the dead branch of this old oak tree could break off in a storm like this, the branches of other trees could do the same thing, and if anybody happened to be under the tree at the time . . .

We both kept calling and yelling.

Then we made a dive outside the tent to the station wagon, but there wasn't anybody there. So we hurried back to the tent again, calling and yelling, trying to make ourselves heard above the roar of the wind and the rain and the thunder, which kept crashing all around us all the time. But we didn't hear any answer.

12

While we were still looking into that part of the tent that was still standing, it seemed good not to have rain beating down on my face and bare head.

In a quick look around, I noticed, even in the dim light, the interesting camp equipment—a three-burner camp stove, a metal roll-away bed, and a roll-away table on which was a pad of writing paper and a flashlight. Also on the table was a kerosene lantern, which was probably the one Mrs. Everhard had been using the night we had seen her digging in the old cemetery beside Sarah Paddler's tombstone. Hanging from one of the leaning tent poles was a religious calendar with a picture of the Good Samaritan on it, showing the man who had gone down from Jerusalem to Jericho and had fallen among thieves, who had robbed him and left him half dead. The man was getting his wounds bound up by the Good Samaritan.

For just a second it seemed I myself was trying to be a Good Samaritan and couldn't be because the person I was trying to be a Good Samaritan to was lost and I couldn't find her.

I hoped that when we did find Charlotte Ann and Mrs. Everhard they wouldn't be half dead, as the man in the Bible story was.

I also noticed that some of the numbers of the calendar had circles around them, which somebody had made with a red pencil or red ink. Without thinking, I said, "That's a pretty picture on that calendar."

Mr. Everhard must not have heard me, because he looked all around and said above the roar of the storm, "The shovel's gone! She's gone out to dig again. Let's go find her, quick!"

As much as I wanted to help find Mrs. Everhard, I was worrying most about Charlotte Ann. So I said, "What about my little sister?"

"Look," he said then, "she's left a note!" He picked up the pad of paper, shone the flashlight on his wife's handwriting, and started in reading, with me looking over his elbow. I know it wasn't polite to do it, but I did it anyway, because the note might have had something in it about Charlotte Ann. This is what it said:

Dearest,

I had another one of my spells, and when I came to myself I was digging over near the rail fence across from the Collins house. I was still very depressed. But when I looked up, I saw dear little Charlotte Ann toddling out across the road all by herself. The minute I saw her, all the clouds in my mind cleared away, and I felt immediately happy.

The little darling was all alone. I took her back across the road to the house, but there was no one at home. I couldn't understand why they would go away and leave her all alone, but it was her nap time, and I thought maybe Bill might have gone to bring us a jug of water, so I brought her back with me to camp.

I think we will go across the north road today because I want to see if I can hear the wood thrush again down by the swamp. If we don't get back soon, and you want to follow us, you will know where to look. I have mastered the wood thrush song at last, so I will have a new whistle from now on. Besides, the turtledove is a little mournful for one who is beginning to be happy.

All my love,
Fran

It was a very nice letter for a woman to write to her husband, I thought. When I'd finished, I liked both of them better. In fact, for a minute I had a kind of homesick feeling in my heart as if I wished there was somebody in the world, besides the gang and my parents, who liked *me*.

But I didn't have time to wish anything for long. An even worse worry startled me into some fast action, for I remembered that the path on the other side of the north road, if you followed it far enough, not only led to the swamp but went on through it. It is the path the gang always takes to go to Old Man Paddler's cabin in the hills, and about twenty feet to the left of the path, as it goes through the swamp, is some quicksand.

Maybe you remember the dark night when Little Tom Till's dad got lost in the swamp and sank down into the mire all the way up to his chin. When our flashlights found him out there, all we could see was his scared face and head, and it looked like a man's head lying in the swamp.

"We've really got to hurry now," I said to Mr. Everhard and told him why. "They probably got as far as the swamp before the storm struck. But it's so dark down there in that part of the woods that they couldn't see the path, and maybe they will get out into the swamp. *Quick!*" I exclaimed. "Let's go!"

I didn't wait for him to decide to follow me but swung around and flung open the flopping tent flap. The two of us dashed out into the storm.

To get to the swamp as quickly as possible was the most important thing in the world.

We stumbled our excited, rain-blinded way toward the Sugar Creek bridge, where our path crossed the north road. I led the way, being careful to keep out in the open so we wouldn't run the risk of getting struck by falling trees or branches. I also stayed away from the tallest trees and especially the tall oak trees, which are the kind of tree lightning strikes more than any other kind.

I won't even take time to tell you more about that wild, worried race. All the way, though, I was hoping that we would get there in time to save Charlotte Ann and Mrs. Everhard from getting out into the swamp itself. I was remembering something Dad had taught me and was also trying to teach Mom. "It's better for your mind to hope something bad *won't* happen than it is to worry about how terrible it would be if it *did*." So I kept one part of my mind saying to the other part, *Why don't you quit worrying and just hope everything will be all right like I do?*

And do you know what? That crazy part of my mind just kept right on worrying anyway.

Over the north road fence, across the road, up the incline, around the end post of another fence, and along the creek we ran. I didn't even notice the different kinds of bushes and wildflowers that bordered the path as I generally do, such as the purple vervain and skullcap and the red-flowered bee comb.

I wouldn't have even noticed the tall mullein stalks with their pretty little yellow, five-petaled flowers if I hadn't run *ker-plop* into one and fallen head over heels, getting my right big toe hurt at the same time.

I was trying to keep my eyes peeled for a little aqua-colored sunsuit, which would be sopping wet, and I suppose Mr. Everhard was looking for some color or other of a dress or a pair of slacks his wife might be wearing.

After what seemed like a week but couldn't have been a half hour, or even a quarter of one, we came to the hollow sycamore tree at the edge of the swamp, where the gang had had so many exciting experiences that you maybe already know about. But there wasn't any sign of Charlotte Ann or Mrs. Everhard. We were still gasping and panting and calling in every direction, but there wasn't any answer.

Then I saw something that made me almost lose control of all my thoughts. The big oak tree that grew on the other side of the path from the sycamore, not more than twenty feet away, had a big, ugly, whitish gash running from its roots all the way up to about twenty feet. The rest of the tree had broken off and fallen, and its branches lay sprawled across the path, right where anybody who might have been in the path at the time would have been struck and smashed into the ground.

That could mean only one thing: Charlotte Ann and Mrs. Everhard would be on the other side of the fallen tree, in the swamp itself, or wandering around on this side somewhere, or else they were under the fallen tree.

I hope they're not *under the tree,* I made myself think, and I yelled for them some more, without getting any answer.

Right that second there was a lull in the storm, when there was no thunder, and the drenching rain almost stopped, and I knew that if it was like some other Sugar Creek storms, it might soon be over.

And then, right in the middle of my worry, I heard the most beautiful music—a flutelike birdcall that was so exactly like the song of a wood thrush—or a brown thrasher, as some folks call that sweet-singing bird—that I thought for sure it was one. A second later, when I heard it again, I knew it *wasn't,* because a thrush wouldn't be very likely to sing its thrilling song in the middle of a summer storm.

Then I remembered what Mrs. Everhard had written to her husband on the note she had left on the roll-away table in the twisted-up tent.

Mr. Everhard must have remembered, too, because he cupped his hands to his lips to protect them from the wind and the rain and whistled back a clear, beautiful quail call. *"Bob White! Bob White! Poor Bob White!"*

And right away there was a cheerful wood thrush answer. It seemed to be saying, *"Lottle-lee. Lottle-lee. Charlotte Ann. Charlotte Ann."* It sounded so cheerful that all of a sudden my heart was as light as a feather. I was pretty sure that if Mrs. Everhard felt happy enough to whistle, Charlotte Ann was safe and all right.

Then I heard another sound coming from Mr. Everhard beside me. It was something I probably wasn't supposed to hear, but it seemed even prettier than a quail or thrush song. Anyway, it must have sounded fine to God. He said, "Thank you, Lord, for sparing her! I'll try to keep my promise."

I remembered that the Bible says there is rejoicing in heaven over one sinner that repents, and it seemed Mr. Everhard had just done that. That is how I knew his prayer, coming out of a rainstorm, would sound awfully pretty to God and maybe to a whole flock of angels who had heard it. In fact, they might have been listening for it, hoping to hear it.

The thrush's song hadn't come from the direction of the swamp, either, where the fallen oak tree was, but from the other side of the sycamore tree in the direction of the Sugar Creek cave. And my heart leaped with the happiest joy I had felt in a long time, when I realized that the song might have come from the cave itself, which, as you know, is a shortcut to Old Man Paddler's cabin in the hills.

I was remembering that the cave is about twelve feet across, not quite as big as the sitting room at our house. I also remembered that Old Man Paddler kept a little desk there and a bench and a few candles. The gang sometimes met there when we were in that part of the woods. We had even stayed almost all night there once—both ends of the night, anyway. The middle of it had been interrupted by Poetry's homemade ghost, which scared the living daylights out of most of the gang.

I yelled to Mr. Everhard, "Come on! They're safe! Hurrah!" I started on a fast, wet run toward the sycamore tree, swerved around it, and went on toward the mouth of the cave itself.

Just as I got there, I noticed that the door, which had been locked for a few weeks, was open. And then, what to my wondering eyes should appear but Mrs. Everhard, wearing the swallowtail butterfly dress I had liked so well that other afternoon when she had borrowed Charlotte Ann. Charlotte Ann herself was standing in front of Mrs. Everhard with one of her chubby hands clasped in hers.

"Come on in out of the rain! Come on in!" Mrs. Everhard said cheerfully. "Mr. Paddler has invited us to come up through the cave to his cabin for a cup of sassafras tea."

13

I tell you, a wonderful feeling started to gallop up and down my spine and all through me as we two drowned rats hurried to the cave and went inside, where it was so quiet we could hardly hear the storm.

"We got here just before the storm broke," Mrs. Everhard said to her husband—and probably also to me.

I noticed that the rock-walled room was all lit up with five or six candles, and then I noticed that over in a corner, sitting at the desk, was Old Man Paddler himself! His long white whiskers reached almost down to his belt, and his hair was white as a summer afternoon cloud in the southwest sky.

I noticed also that there were several new, comfortable chairs in the cave, the kind that people have in their houses. Over on the east wall, hanging from a wooden peg that was driven into a crack, was a beautiful wall motto, *"God causes all things to work together for good to those who love God."*

So this is why he has had the cave closed up for the past few weeks, I thought. He had closed it for repairs, the way they do a store in town when they are redecorating it. It was really pretty neat.

"How do you like our reception room?" Mrs. Everhard asked her husband.

He stared at her.

Knowing he didn't understand what she meant, she said, "Today was my consultation day, you know. Mr. Paddler has been giving me lessons in faith, teaching me how to trust everything to God and . . ."

While she was talking, I noticed that Charlotte Ann was hiding herself behind Mrs. Everhard's skirts the way she does behind Mom's sometimes when she feels bashful.

Then Mr. Everhard asked a question. "You mean you have been coming here for *consultations*?"

"Every other day for over a week. I had a hard time sneaking away sometimes, but I managed it—while you thought I was at the Collinses and once when you thought I was taking a nap. But I won't have to come anymore."

Her voice suddenly broke, and I could tell that some tears had gotten into it. Then, maybe not realizing that her husband's clothes were as wet as a soaked sponge and that she had on her pretty swallowtail butterfly dress, she made a dive for him, sobbing and saying, "Oh, John, darling! I see it now! I see it! God is good! God *does* love me, and I *know* we will see our dear little Elsa again in heaven! I have learned to trust! There is rest in heaven, as it says on Sarah Paddler's tombstone!"

It was a sight I maybe wasn't supposed to see. I noticed that Old Man Paddler himself got out a snow-white handkerchief and brushed away a couple of tears. Then he adjusted his thick-lensed glasses and looked down at the Bible on the desk in front of him.

"Just this afternoon," Mrs. Everhard said with her face buried against her husband's neck, "when I saw the clouds rolling and twisting and I knew there was going to be a bad storm, I was so afraid for little Charlotte Ann. I prayed and prayed as I ran, knowing if I could get here, we would be safe. When lightning struck that old tree out there, and it came crashing down in the very place where we had been just a moment before, I realized that God Himself was looking after us. So I began to thank Him. And without knowing I was going to do it, I was also thanking Jesus for dying upon the cross for me that my sins might be forgiven and—and all of a sudden I began to be very happy inside. Oh, John!"

Mrs. Everhard stopped talking and just clung to her husband. They stood with their arms around each other, and little Charlotte Ann stood below them, not knowing what was going on at all.

Then Charlotte Ann looked up at them and, as she does sometimes when Mom and Dad are standing like that, she beat her little hands on Mrs. Everhard's knees and said to them in her cute little baby voice, "I want to be up where the heads are."

Well, that is the beginning of the end of

this story about one of the most wonderful things that ever happened around Sugar Creek.

After the storm was over and the clouds had cleared away and the friendly sun was shining again on a terribly wet world that had just had a good rainwater bath, we said good-bye to Old Man Paddler, not accepting his kind invitation to go through the cave to his cabin for a cup of sassafras tea. I knew I had better get back home with Charlotte Ann before my parents got there, so that when they did get there I would just be finishing my job of two hours of baby-sitting.

I maybe ought to close the windows, too. And if there was any rainwater on the floor anywhere, I had better get it mopped up quick before Dad or Mom or both of them at the same time saw it and started mopping up on me.

We were all the way to the Sugar Creek bridge when Mr. Everhard stopped to say, "Where's the shovel you took with you when you left the tent?"

Mrs. Everhard laughed a very musical laugh and answered, "I gave it to Mr. Paddler. He needs a new one for his flower garden up in the hills. Besides, I don't think I'll ever need it again. Will I, darling?" she said to Charlotte Ann, whom she was carrying.

But Charlotte Ann didn't seem to understand what it was all about. "I'm hungry," she said.

Just that second there was a rippling bird voice from somewhere in the woods, and it sounded like *"O Lottle-lee. Lottle-lee."* It was an honest-to-goodness wood thrush this time, which probably felt extrahappy about something now that the storm was over.

When we got to the green tent, Mrs. Everhard just stood looking at all the damage the storm had done. In fact, none of us said anything for a minute, not even Charlotte Ann. I was sort of expecting her to make some kind of a woman's exclamation and feel terribly bad. But instead she said quietly, "Well, that's that. It was God's storm, so we'll have to accept what it did to our property." And I thought what a wonderful teacher Old Man Paddler had been.

Then she seemed to forget that Charlotte Ann and I were there, because she said, "It's been a wonderful vacation, John, *wonderful!* I'll never be able to thank God enough for such a thoughtful husband and for that dear old man in the cave."

Well, I can't take time now to tell you any more about what happened that day, except that I did get home with Charlotte Ann at just about the time my folks drove up to our mailbox. Mom was so thankful we were all right that she didn't say much about the rainwater on the kitchen floor and my wet clothes.

Besides, the Everhards were there, and it seems Mom thinks I am a better boy when we have company than when we don't. Also, Mr. Everhard was all wet, too, and it might not seem right for a boy to get a scolding for something it was all right for a grown-up to do.

The Everhards couldn't stay in their tent that night, so Little Jim's mom kept them at their house, for they have one of the best spare rooms in all the Sugar Creek territory. Tomorrow the bobwhite and his wood thrush wife could move back into the tent, after it had been dried out and pitched in a new and better location.

Big Jim himself picked out the best campsite in the woods for the Everhards, and with some of our dads helping a little, we moved the tent and all their equipment about fifty feet from the linden tree.

Then we called a special gang meeting to talk over all the exciting things that had happened, especially to Charlotte Ann and the turtledove—who had turned into a wood thrush—and her bobwhite husband.

We spent maybe an hour walking around through the woods to see how many trees had been blown down or uprooted. Some of our favorite trees had, which made us feel kind of sad. But it was good to be together even though we couldn't go in swimming.

Sugar Creek's ordinarily nice, clear, friendly water was an angry-looking brown and was running almost as fast along its course as it does all the time just in the riffles. Both ends of the bayou were so full they came together in the middle to make one big, long pond, and I thought about how sad the cute little barred pickerel must feel to have their playground spoiled for them. It certainly wouldn't be much fun for them to have to look at everything through muddy water. Besides, who wants to have muddy water in his eyes all the time?

There wasn't very much we could do that was exciting enough for a gang of boys, and we couldn't even lie down and roll in the grass. It was still wet.

"We can all go home and help our folks— maybe offer to hoe potatoes or something," Poetry said with a heavy sigh.

Circus answered, "It's too wet to work the ground today. Don't you know that?"

"Sure I know that," Poetry answered with a grin. "That's why I said it."

"What *can* we do?" Dragonfly asked in a discouraged, whining voice.

It was Little Tom Till who thought of something that sounded interesting. "Let's all go down to the cave and see the way Old Man Paddler has fixed it up."

"Yeah," Little Jim chimed in, "and let's go through it up to his cabin and see if maybe he will offer to make us some sassafras tea."

From the old linden tree, where we were at the time, we rambled toward the bridge, following the shore of the creek, which certainly didn't look friendly today, even with the cheerful afternoon sun shining down on it. I wished everything would hurry up and get back to normal. If there is anything in the world that gives a person a sad feeling, it is to have his favorite swimming hole spoiled by a heavy rain.

"Ho-hum," I sighed as I was climbing over the rail fence at the north road.

"Ho-hum, yourself," Poetry sighed back at me.

Only Little Jim seemed happy. He was standing on the top rail of the fence. "What you guys so sad for?"

"Sad?" I answered. "Who's sad?"

"Yeah, who is?" Big Jim said sadly.

"What are *you* grinning like a possum for?" Dragonfly asked Little Jim.

The little fellow scooted down the other side of the fence then, saying over his shoulder as he ran across the gravel road, "Because next winter I get to go to the Everhards' new resort at Squaw Lake and go ice fishing. And I can take two of the gang along with me, whichever two of you want to go. They just bought a resort up there last week and are going to move there this fall."

Little Jim had found out all that while the Everhards had been at his house. He was halfway over the fence on the other side of the road when he finished telling us about it.

Well, this has got to be the last part of this story, because I have to get started as quick as I can on the next one—a long and happy and exciting story about how *all* the gang got to go to the Everhards' resort in the wilds of the North for a few days' ice fishing, up where there were a lot of wild animals living all around in the forest. Talk about a different kind of fun and also a different kind of adventure! Boy oh boy!

I'll finish this by telling you something that happened that afternoon when we got to the cave.

"Hurry up," Little Jim called to us.

And for some reason, his cheerful voice made me begin to feel wonderful as we all swished across the road, up the embankment on the other side, and started on a helter-skelter gallop toward the cave—*where we found an envelope tacked to the door.*